I0537846

Lauren Mills has never gone home with a stranger, but she cannot resist the handsome man who has just rescued her from her cheating ex-boyfriend. Something in Sawyer Scott's eyes touches her heart and sets her body on fire. But she knows it can only be one night. Her life, delayed by the tragic death of her parents, begins in the morning in a new city, a new house, and a new job. Can she let go of her past? Can she open her heart to a new future?

The unauthorized reproduction or distribution of this copy-righted work is illegal. Criminal copyright infringement, including infringement without monetary gain, is investigated by the FBI and is punishable by up to 5 years in federal prison and a fine of $250,000.

This book is a work of fiction. Names, characters, places, and incidents either are products of the author's imagination or are used fictitiously. Any resemblance to actual events or locales or persons, living or dead, is entirely coincidental.

An Apple A Day
Copyright © 2019 Kandeis Lynne
ISBN: 978-1-4874-2684-2
Cover art by Martine Jardin

All rights reserved. Except for use in any review, the reproduction or utilization of this work in whole or in part in any form by any electronic, mechanical or other means, now known or hereafter invented, is forbidden without the written permission of the publisher.

Published by eXtasy Books Inc or
Devine Destinies, an imprint of eXtasy Books Inc

Look for us online at:
www.eXtasybooks.com or www.devinedestinies.com

An Apple A Day Reading, Writing, and Erotica, Book 2

By

Kandeis Lynne

DEDICATION

Among other things, this story is about best friends. I have been lucky to have many in my life. This book is for my best friends, and all the other best friends, who would provide an alibi with no questions asked.

Chapter One: Last Chance to Dance

"Come on. We're going to be late. Matt's set starts at eight." Dani Alonzo drummed her manicured nails impatiently on the stair banister.

Lauren Mills sighed and mumbled, "I'm coming. I'm coming." Pursing her lips, she quickly applied a coat of pale lip gloss. At the bottom of the stairs, she checked her blonde hair in the mirror a final time. Her straight ash blonde hair was twisted in a classic, casual chignon. Her high cheekbones and blue eyes needed little in the way of cosmetics. She only wore makeup to make herself look older. At twenty-four, Lauren could have easily passed for sixteen. Lauren remembered the times her mother had promised *you'll be glad you look so young someday*. But Lauren was seldom glad to look so young. She wasn't taken seriously. The boys who asked her out still had acne, while the men closer to her age assumed that she was jailbait and off limits.

"You look perfect. Now come on," Dani teased. "This is our last chance to go dancing before you start your new job."

Daniella Marguerite Sophia Alonzo, Lauren's best friend and partner in crime since elementary school, was the perfect foil to Lauren's pale coloring and willowy height. Barely five feet with high heels, she had classic Mediterranean coloring. Her dark skin suited her unruly mop of dark curls and sultry features. While Lauren needed very little makeup, Dani skillfully used cosmetics to accentuate her dark eyes and full lips.

1

Pausing to hug her friend, Lauren promised, "It's not like I'm moving to the moon, I'm only going to be a few hours away. We can still hang out. I'll come back to visit, and you can come stay with me anytime you want."

"I know, but it just won't be the same," Dani declared with a sigh.

"Look at it this way. You'll always have a free place to stay at the beach."

She and Dani had been best friends for as long as she could remember. When her parents had unexpectedly died in a car wreck when Lauren was only seventeen, the Alonzos had taken her in. They were closer than sisters. Lauren looked at her best friend and felt tears welling in her eyes. *Am I making a mistake moving away?* She had worked hard to get her teaching credentials. Her dream job was waiting a few hours away. She knew she had to go, but she would miss her friend desperately.

"Hey now, don't you start boohooing!" Dani admonished when Lauren dabbed at her eyes.

Lost in her own thoughts, Lauren was startled when Dani asked, "Do you think Nick will be at the club tonight?

Nick.

He was another reason she had to go. Nicholas Weaver has been the love of her life for the past four years. She had always assumed they would get married and have beautiful fat babies with his dark hair and her big blue eyes — that was, until she had found him in bed with the red-headed cashier from the Quickie Mart three months ago. *Quickie, indeed.* Friends had been amazed at how well she had handled the situation. She hadn't raged. She hadn't screamed. She had just calmly told him to get his things and leave. She had refused all his attempts to talk to her. Dani had been the only witness to her true fury as she smashed everything Nick had ever given her. And when she had collapsed in gut-wrenching tears on her couch, Dani had quietly swept up the glass, torn photos, and eviscerated stuffed animals.

"God, I hope not," Lauren swore aloud. She wanted to believe that she was over him, but that didn't mean that she was ready to come face to face with him.

The club was crowded by the time Lauren and Dani weaved their way through the bar to order drinks—a margarita on the rocks with salt for Lauren and a rum and coke for Dani. Predictably, the bartender carded Lauren. Dani hadn't been asked for identification since she was fourteen. Big breasts and a curvy figure made men automatically assume she was older. Lauren was prepared and handed over her driver's license.

Gesturing toward the rear of the club, Dani shouted, "Hey, I see a table in the back. I'm going to go claim it before someone else does." Lauren gave Dani an okay sign as she began to negotiate her way through the crowd.

"Here you go," the bartender announced, sliding the two drinks across the bar.

Balancing the two drinks and basket of pretzels high above the surging mass of people, Lauren made her way to the small table. Laughing, she shouted, "Good grief. It's a madhouse in here tonight." But Dani's response was lost as the band began to tune their instruments.

Matt Marsh bounded onto the stage to the cheers of the frenzied crowd. He was a stereotypical beach boy right down to his board shorts and Hawaiian print shirt. His band, *Squirrel Army*, covered beach songs by artists like Jimmy Buffett, Bob Marley, and The Beach Boys. The band was popular and was booked months in advance. Matt was doing well enough to have bought the flashy diamond engagement ring that sparkled on Dani's left hand. While he wasn't Lauren's type, he was exactly Dani's type—tan and muscular with the blatant sexuality of a rock star. Nonetheless, Lauren really liked Matt. He was sweet, kind, and completely devoted to Dani, and that was good enough for her.

She and Dani had rarely had the same taste in men. Dani preferred the obvious blond cocksure artistic type, while Lauren's taste ran more to the dark mysterious tortured souls. That wasn't to say that they had never liked the same guy, but usually one of them called dibs and the other backed off. There had, however, been one young man that had almost come between them—Grayson Park. Grayson had been Lauren's first real boyfriend. She had been fifteen and in love with a capital L. She had blithely gone to summer camp assuming he would put his teenage hormones on ice until she got back. Unfortunately, Dani had been in his line of sight when young Grayson decided that he couldn't wait any longer. Dani and Grayson had made out in the backseat of his Camaro after a party. Guilty and remorseful, Dani had confessed to Lauren as soon as she returned from camp. After a few angry tears, Lauren forgave her. Neither of them ever forgave Grayson.

Lauren barely had time to set the drinks down before Dani shouted, "Come on. Let's dance." Dani was an enthusiastic and athletic dancer, but Lauren had always felt too self-conscious. While Dani danced with wild abandon, Lauren generally stuck to the step-tap-step-tap until she was drunk enough to stop worrying about how she looked and just enjoyed herself. Tonight, she had every intention of enjoying herself.

Between songs, Lauren made her way back to the table to gulp down her margarita and order another round. The drink went down easily, the tequila burning in her empty stomach. Lauren wrinkled her nose in distaste as Dani sipped her rum and coke. "How can you drink that stuff?"

"I don't know. I guess I just got used to it."

Dani snorted with laughter. "Do you remember when my parents left us alone for a weekend and we got completely pissed on coconut rum?"

"Are you kidding? To this day, I can't drink anything with rum in it. Even the smell makes my stomach turn."

By the time the band took a break, Lauren was buzzed. She liked the freedom that she felt when she was intoxicated. Tequila lowered her inhibitions and allowed her to be the person she wanted to be instead of the strait-laced, inhibited good girl that people saw. She wanted to be wild and reckless. She wanted to flirt and laugh and dance. She wanted to feel alive.

Matt made his way from the stage to join them. Kissing Lauren on the top of the head and Dani on the lips, he pulled a chair out and straddled it backward.

"You guys sound amazing tonight," Lauren offered.

"Thanks. So, are you all packed for the big city?"

"I guess so. There wasn't that much to move. The furniture's on its way on the moving truck, and my clothes are piled in the back of my car. That's all there is, really."

"I like it" — Matt laughed — "a girl who travels light."

"Have you seen her car?" Dani objected. "I don't know how she can see to drive."

Laughing, Matt reached for Dani's hand. "Hey, I've got a little problem that I could use some help with. You want to step out back for a few minutes before I go on stage again?"

Snorting in laughter, Dani asked, "Seriously?"

"What can I say? Being a rock star makes me horny."

"Save my seat, I'll only be gone a minute — maybe two," Dani teased.

"Ha, ha, ha, you think you are so funny," Matt sarcastically teased as he pulled Dani to her feet and lead her to the back exit.

"Have fun." Lauren watched a little wistfully as her friend disappeared. Lauren knew what Matt's *little problem* was. Dani had described in detail Matt's between-set quickies. She envied the happy couple. She missed having someone to love. Even more, she missed having someone to fuck. She was just drunk enough to feel needy and frustrated. Self-conscious sitting at the table alone, Lauren decided that she needed another drink. Winding her way through the crowd, Lauren felt several men's hands accidentally brush against her ass. She didn't mind. It made her feel sexy to know that they wanted to touch her. She hadn't been with anyone since Nick, and the alcohol was beginning to stoke a fire in her that left her nipples hard and her panties damp.

CHAPTER TWO: DAMSEL IN DISTRESS

Sawyer had just come in for a quick drink. He hadn't intended to stay, but the band was surprisingly good, and he found the noise and anonymous crowd provided a respite from his thoughts.

Sawyer wasn't looking for company. He wanted to drink and forget. Forget the past. Forget his uncertain future. Forget his name if he could. From his seat at the bar, Sawyer's gaze skimmed the crowd. The bar crowd was typical, lots of beautiful twenty-somethings dancing and drinking as is they would never be forty-somethings, a clutch of older women trying too hard, and the assorted divorcees looking for a hook-up. He was none of those. He was alone and wanted to be left alone. That part of his life was over, and the sooner he accepted it, the better.

He ordered another bourbon and leaned back against the bar to watch the crowd. When a lithe blonde squeezed past him to order another drink, he was surprised at his body's reaction. She wore a gauzy white sundress that dipped dangerously low between her breasts and even further in the back. As he watched her adjusted the slim straps that kept slipping from her shoulders, his mind wandered. He imagined sliding those straps all the way down past her long sexy legs until the dress pooled at her feet. *What is she wearing under that simple white dress?* He imagined sliding his fingers into lacy white panties that stood out against her tanned skin. He imagined drawing nipples that poked through her thin dress into his mouth and sucking them as she moaned.

Sawyer suddenly became aware that his cock had grown hard and was straining against his buttoned fly. What was he thinking? This wasn't a good idea at all. All he needed to add to his misery was a boner with no place to go. Just as he convinced himself to stop fantasizing about the stunning blonde, she looked up at him, and then her blue eyes lasered straight to his groin. Impossibly, he felt himself grow even harder. He watched as she bit her lower lip and lowered her gaze while a blush bloomed across her bare skin. The bartender interrupted his carnal thoughts when he slid her drinks across the bar.

Lifting her glass to drink, Lauren peeked over the salted rim and studied him. The sleeves of his white dress shirt were rolled up to reveal strong, tanned forearms. The expensive shirt stretched across his back, accentuating his broad shoulders, and fell open at the neck, revealing a sprinkle of dark chest hair. His crisp shirt was tucked into dark denim jeans that hung low on his angular hips. A lock of curly black hair fell across his forehead, giving him a cherubic look. But the angelic appearance stopped at his eyes. His gray-blue eyes glinted dangerously. He both frightened and excited her. In spite of herself, she smiled at him.

"Sawyer," he announced as he stood from his barstool.

"Lauren. Nice to meet you, Sawyer."

When she turned to negotiate her way back through the crowd, Sawyer unexpectedly heard himself ask, "Would you like to dance?" *What the hell? Why did I do that? I don't want company. I want to be left alone to soak in my bourbon. Right?* But he couldn't help himself. She was dazzling. Her face was flush with the heat and alcohol. She wore little makeup on her golden skin, and dark lashes smudged her blue eyes. He noted a few grains of salt sitting tantalizingly on her lower lip.

He wanted to lick the salt from her full, ripe lips as he kissed her. A thin sheen of perspiration dewed her shoulders and décolletage. He watched as a bead of moisture slid between her breasts. He wondered if his frank appraisal offended her. She probably should have slapped him for the way he was leering at her. Surprisingly she boldly lifted her head, looked into his eyes, and nodded. Lifting the two drinks, Lauren mimed that she needed to set them down first. Sawyer followed her to the small table and waited as she took a sip of her margarita. He felt his cock twitch as he watched her tongue dart out to lick salt from the rim of her glass.

A slow sexy song began to play over the sound system. He was excited and terrified at the same time. When he reached out to pull her into his arms, he felt a tingle that began where she touched him and spread to all the places that he wanted her to touch. Their bodies melted into one another as if they had been made for dancing together.

Sawyer tried to turn off his brain. He didn't want to think about anything. He just wanted to feel this beautiful woman moving with him. More accurately, Sawyer turned off all rational thoughts. He was definitely having some quite irrational thoughts about what he wanted to do with this woman. He could feel her lithe body through her thin white dress. She certainly couldn't help but be aware that he was enjoying holding her close. His body had made that clear the moment they embraced.

Unfortunately, there was a difference between what he *wanted* to do and what he *would* do. When the music slowed, they stood, still embracing. It would have been so easy to kiss her. She was there in his arms, her face turned up to his, her lips parted and inviting. "Thank you, Lauren," he whispered as he forced himself to release her. She stood speechless as he turned and walked away from her.

"Who was that?" Dani shouted emphatically over the music as Lauren joined her.

"Who?" Lauren asked, feigning innocence.

"What do you mean who? Mister Tall, Dark, and Dreamy."

"I think he said his name was Sawyer."

"You think?" Dani asked, eyes wide with sarcasm. "Are you blind, deaf, and dumb, child? He's fucking gorgeous."

Lauren dared a glance back toward Sawyer but was disappointed to discover that he was no longer seated at the bar. "It doesn't matter anyway. He's gone." She was surprised at the pang of loss she felt. Sure, he was attractive, but she had seen something else flit across his features, a longing that spoke to her even deeper. As she turned her gaze back to her friend, Lauren spotted Nick's familiar dark head above the crowd.

"Oh shit. Nick's here."

Dani pleaded, "Just ignore him. Don't talk to him. Don't even acknowledge him." Lauren was weak where Nick was concerned. The latest romp with the Quickie Mart cashier wasn't the first time Nick had cheated on Lauren, nor was it the first time she had caught him. Lauren had finally stood up to Nick and thrown him out, but tonight Lauren was drunk and vulnerable.

"Maybe he won't come over," Lauren said hopefully.

"Too late. Here he comes."

Dani stepped in front of Lauren to intercept Nick, but Lauren reached out and pulled her friend back. "Don't worry, Dani. I've got this."

CHAPTER THREE: IT'S ALWAYS BEEN YOU

Nick was six-four and one-hundred-eighty pounds of muscle and ego. His straight dark hair swooped to one side above luxurious eyelashes that any girl would have killed for. His sensual brown eyes and full lips oozed sex appeal. His snug white t-shirt accentuated his muscular shoulders and arms. He was beautiful. Every woman in the bar watched him as he strolled confidently across the floor.

Nick leaned in close to speak to Lauren.

She shivered when his mouth brushed her ear.

"Hey, can we talk?"

Lauren braced herself mentally. "No. I have nothing to say to you."

"I'm sorry. I just thought. I don't expect you to forgive me. I just hoped maybe we could still be friends."

Everything he said sounded so reasonable when he said it. *Is it unreasonable for me to refuse to be friends?* But she knew how the conversation would go. By the end of the evening, she would be apologizing and comforting *him*. Somehow, he always managed to make her feel like she was the one who had done something wrong.

Not this time! Her heart ached for the man that she had loved most of her adult life, but she knew that she had to avoid his narcissistic spider web. She had to shut him down. She had to cut him out of her life completely this time. There was no halfway with Nicholas Weaver. You either loved him or you hated him, and to survive, she needed to hate him.

"No, Nick. Please go away."

"Lauren, baby, you know that girl meant nothing to me. I love you. It's always been you," Nick wheedled.

Weakly Lauren said, "Nick, please don't do this."

"Lauren, I thought you were different." Flattery was one of Nick's most seductive ploys. He would manipulate her emotions until she tried to live up to his expectations.

As Lauren began to waver, Dani interrupted. "Nick. She doesn't want to talk to you. Get lost!" As Nick turned to unleash a few choice words about Dani minding her own business, Lauren spied Sawyer making his way toward their table.

"Are you ready to go, sweetheart?" Sawyer asked, casually draping his arm around her bare shoulder. Momentarily stupefied, Lauren stood staring at Sawyer.

Much quicker on her feet, Dani stepped in. "Sawyer, honey, you'll make sure she gets home safe?"

"Of course. Don't I always?" Sawyer replied smoothly. Nick watched speechlessly as Sawyer gently guided Lauren toward the door.

Outside the club, the cool night air snapped Lauren out of her daze. "Oh my God! Thank you. I can't believe you just did that."

"You seemed like you needed a knight in shining armor."

"That was amazing. Did you see his face? And Dani? She totally played along."

"Can I assume that you *did* want to be rescued?"

"Most definitely," she said, looking up at him.

With the adrenaline rush of their escape fading, they stood awkwardly looking at each other in the streetlight. She was becoming uncomfortably aware of him. She could feel the heat from his skin where his arm still rested on her shoulder. Even the smell of him was causing delicious ripples to move through her body. Her taut nipples rubbed tantalizingly against her gauzy dress. She pressed her thighs together to quiet the pressure that was growing between her legs.

"I guess I better call a cab. I can't go back in there."

"I could take you home," Sawyer offered casually.

"But I don't—" The rest of Lauren's words were cut off when his mouth descended upon hers. Tentative at first, he groaned when she opened her lips to his. Pulling her against his length, he devoured her with his mouth. As he thrust his tongue into her mouth, she imagined his cock thrusting into her. When she moaned against him, he slid his hands lower on her back until he was cupping her ass. Lifting her slightly, he pulled her tight against him so that she could feel his arousal.

"Sawyer." Lauren sighed against his mouth.

The sound of his name on her lips nearly pushed him over the edge. He wanted to hear her scream his name as he made her come around him. Somewhere in the back of his mind was a little voice pointing out what a bad idea this was, but the louder voice was in his dick. He slid one hand between them to stroke the nipples that had been teasing him all night.

"Would you like to go back to my place?" he whispered. In reply, Lauren reached between them and drew one long finger along his erection. Thankfully, his house was only a few minutes away. When he settled uncomfortably behind the steering wheel, she snuggled close to him. As he attempted to obey traffic laws, she unbuttoned his jeans and slid her fingers into his boxers to stroke his throbbing cock. At a stop light, he became so engrossed in kissing her that he missed the green light. Reaching his house, he adjusted his clothing and helped her from the car.

When she reached up to slide her thumb across his nipple,

he gave up any semblance of propriety and threw her over his shoulder. He carried her, giggling, up the stairs and lowered her to her feet. She hadn't seen much of the rest of the house from her position over his shoulder, but the bedroom was bare except for a massive king-sized bed and a handful of packing boxes. He turned on a single lamp sitting forlornly in a corner, then sat on the edge of the bed in front of her. She stood for a moment, silent, eyes downcast. Mistaking her silence for second thoughts, he offered, "You know if you've changed your mind . . ."

In answer, she slid the straps of her dress off her shoulders and allowed the flimsy material to fall to the floor.

She was breathtaking. Her tanned skin was flawless. He reached up to place his palm against her flat sun-kissed belly. As he slid his hand to her hips, he noticed a bikini tan line. Dragging his fingers deliciously up her sides to her breasts, he noticed with a grin, no tan lines there. Lowering his mouth, he pulled one ripe nipple between his lips and slid his tongue over the sensitive tip. Lauren's head fell back as she arched into him. While lavishing the other breast with the same attention, he slid one hand between her legs. God, she was soft and wet. He slid her lacy panties down her legs. Standing, he reversed their positions, so she sat on the edge of the bed. Lowering himself to his knees, he nudged her legs apart. Slowly he dragged a finger across her wet crease, causing her to whimper. He watched her eyes widen as he drew his finger into his mouth to taste her sweetness. Without breaking eye contact, he slid his wet finger into her. He was gratified to see her mouth fall open. He slid a second finger into her, filling her. He heard her cry out when his calloused thumb found her clit. As he felt her tightening around him, she abruptly reached out and stopped him.

"You still have on too many clothes," she said huskily.

"Why don't you do something about that?" he dared her.

14

Lauren stood, completely comfortable in her nudity, and reached for his shirt. Achingly slowly she undid the buttons, scorching him every time her fingers brushed his bare skin. Sliding his shirt off his shoulders, she lowered herself to her knees. Undoing the buttons he had hastily rebuttoned earlier, she allowed his pants to join her dress on the floor. She quickly added his boxers to the pile. Slowly, she drew one finger along his erect cock. Sawyer felt his knees quiver as his dick jerked in response to her touch. She looked up at him through a thick fringe of lashes and licked her lips. Grasping his balls with one hand, she drew his cock into her soft hot mouth.

Sawyer saw stars. He honest to God saw stars. He couldn't hear anything but the blood pounding in his ears. "Oh God," he moaned as she drew him in deeper to her throat. His hips rocked into her rhythmically against his will. He wouldn't last if she kept this up.

Shakespeare. Think about Shakespeare.

Some guys thought about math. Others thought about baseball. He recited Shakespeare.

To be or not to be, that is the question. Whether 'tis nobler in the mind to suffer. His concentration wavered as Lauren added her teeth to the unbearable friction she was applying to his cock. Alas, poor Yorick. I knew him, Fellatio — no — I knew him, Horatio.

Lauren paused and looked up as she heard him snort in laughter. Realizing he had disrupted the moment, he reached down and pulled her to her feet. "I, uhm, I hate to — it's kind of late to mention this, but I don't have any . . ." He gestured helplessly around the nearly empty room. The truth was he wouldn't have had any condoms even if his house wasn't nearly packed. He hadn't needed them before, and it had never occurred to him that he might ever need them again. It had been a really, long time — his daughter's whole lifetime.

"I think I might have one," Lauren offered, looking around for her purse.

Jesus, what kind of woman has condoms in her purse?

Lauren located her purse and stepped closer to the lamp to dig through it. In the process, she glanced at her phone and read the four increasingly frantic messages from Dani.

Nick left. Where are you? – happy face emoji.

Lauren, did you leave? Let me know where you are? – no emoji.

Lo', I'm starting to freak out here. Where are you? Did you leave with Sawyer? Do I need to come rescue you?

What the fuck? Call me.

Lauren sent a quick message assuring Dani that she was fine. Feeling a little guilty for worrying her friend, she added *sorry* and a kissing smiley face emoji. She *was* fine. Hooking up with a total stranger wasn't something she normally did. Well, to be honest, it wasn't something she had ever done. *But I am fine, right?* Sawyer had gallantly rescued her from Nick. His cowboy hat was white. He was the good guy.

Lauren turned to admire Sawyer, who lay resting on one elbow watching her. The light from the single lamp high-lighted the angularity of his lean, muscular body. In the dim light, he looked a little less like a knight in shining armor and little more like a dangerous animal. On second thought, Lauren tapped, *share my location.* She was here by choice—but just in case.

The phone pinged back almost as fast as she hit send. Lauren was relieved to see Dani was going to leave her car in front of Sawyer's house. At least she had a way to get home now.

"Everything okay with your friend?" Sawyer asked.

"Sorry," Lauren offered embarrassed, "she worries."

"I don't blame her. She sounds like a good friend."

"She is," Lauren added awkwardly.

Gracefully rising from the bed, Sawyer padded across the

room to stand facing Lauren. "You know, I don't usually —"

"No, I don't either," she interrupted.

Leaning into her so his forehead touched the top of her head, he whispered, "Do you want to stay?"

Lauren tilted her head up to look at him. His eyes were hard, but there was something else there, something fragile. When she nodded, he wrapped his arms around her and lifted her off her feet. She wrapped her legs around his hips as he carried her to the bed. He sat on the edge of the bed with her still straddling him.

Grinning, she held up a condom wrapped in glittery pink foil emblazoned with *Dani and Matt 4-Ever*. "Dani's bachelorette party . . ."

Laughing, he opened it, reached between them, and rolled the condom down his length.

Chapter Four: Jinx, You Owe Me A Soda

Lauren pulled her car into the parking lot of the Oceanside Elementary School. She killed the engine and sat staring at the building. This was her first teaching job. She had spent the last four years of her life preparing for this. She wasn't worried about the teaching part. She had earned a degree in Early Childhood Education. She was certified by the state to teach kindergarten through fourth grade. She had enjoyed her student teaching rotation. She felt confident that this was what she was meant to do with her life. *So why am I so nervous?*

Deep down, though, she knew. This was more than the first day of a new job. This was the first day of her life. Her parents' death had sent her into a tailspin. Between the grief and loss, she had barely passed her last semester of high school. If Daniel and Maria Alonzo hadn't taken her in, she couldn't imagine what would have happened to her. They had kept her safe and fed. They tried to give her the love she missed from her parents. She knew she could never repay them — financially or emotionally. But now she was finally moving forward. She was living the moments that should have happened six years ago. She had left home, Dani, and especially Nick, behind her.

"Well here goes," she murmured to herself as she strode across the parking lot.

With as much confidence and enthusiasm as she could muster, Lauren introduced herself to the older woman buried behind stacks of manila folders. "Hi, I'm Lauren Mills. I'm the new first-grade teacher. I'm supposed to meet with Mister Scott this morning."

"Well, dear, that's going to be a problem. Mister Scott isn't here and won't be for several more days," the older woman announced without looking up.

Deflated, Lauren stood for a moment unsure what to do next. "Well then, I wonder if you could direct me to the first-grade hall."

With obvious annoyance, the harried woman set down the file she was flipping through and said, "Go past the lunch-room, first hall on the left. It's got a big one over it."

"Don't worry about it, Elouise. I'll show her."

Lauren turned to see a gorgeous redhead wearing cutoff denim shorts and a gray Oceanside Elementary Field Day t-shirt.

"Hey, welcome to Oceanside. I'm Rebecca, but everyone calls me Jinx, and this old grouch is Elouise Gilbert, our sec-retary."

"I am not an old grouch," Elouise denied loudly. Con-cerned, Lauren looked back at the older woman, but Elouise had nothing but fondness in her eyes as she looked at Re-becca.

"Come on. I'll give you the nickel tour," Jinx offered as she held the door open for Lauren.

"So, how does Rebecca turn into Jinx?" Lauren asked as they walked down the hall.

"Well, I'm named after my mother, Rebecca, and she was named after my grandmother, Rebecca, and so on, as far as anyone can remember. When my granny was alive, it could get very confusing when someone called out for Rebecca. All three of us would answer. After a while, we started saying *jinx* whenever we all answered. You know, like when some-one says the same thing you say and you say *jinx, you owe me a soda*. Eventually, I just became Jinx. It started as a joke, but it actually made things a lot easier."

Turning down the first hall, Jinx warned, "Don't ever name your children after you. Sometimes, it has been a real hassle." Turning her bright green eyes and infectious smile on Lauren, she amended, "Well, maybe not a hassle, but I was glad enough to become Jinx.

"By the way, don't let Elouise scare you. She's really a big teddy bear. The students adore her. She just gets over-whelmed at the beginning of the year with all the student records. Add to that, Mister Melbourne's retirement and the fact that the new principal won't even be here until after the school starts."

Understanding dawning, Lauren asked, "Let me guess, Mister Scott?"

"Yes. We've heard he's a real hunk, but no one's seen him yet. What do you think?"

"I'm afraid I'm as in the dark as you are. Not only have I never met him, but I've also never even spoken to him. I was hired at a job fair last spring. A couple of weeks ago, I got a letter informing me that Mister Melbourne was retiring, and I should report to Mister Scott."

Opening a classroom door, Jinx motioned for Lauren to enter. "Welcome to your new room."

Lauren spun around to admire her new classroom. Red checked curtains framed a plate glass window across one wall. Sunlight streamed through and glinted off the dust motes in the air. Another corner held a small wooden loft decorated with apple-shaped pillows and painted to look like a tree house perched in an apple tree. Delicate painted blue-birds and butterflies danced across the walls. Painted flowers sprouted from the floorboards. Several large green rugs gave the illusion of grass growing around the small red student chairs. A bulletin board spanning one wall announced, *Ms. Mills Class is the Best in the Bushel.*

"Oh, Jinx, it's beautiful." Lauren sighed.

"Yeah, well," Jinx began sheepishly, "we already had our classrooms set up, so we pitched in and got yours ready. We figured you had enough to do, being a new teacher and all."

"Oh, how can I ever thank you?" Lauren asked with tears in her eyes.

"Don't worry, there's still plenty of work to do," Jinx teased, deflecting Lauren's gratitude.

"Where do I even begin?" Lauren asked as Jinx began pulling out teacher's editions and reading guides for Lauren.

"The new boss wants written lesson plans for the first month of school. You'll need to plan for at least three leveled groups in math, reading, and spelling. We all do a canned writing program, so you don't really have to plan for that — plan for social studies and science at least once a week. Gym, music, art, and swimming are pull-outs. That's when you get a break."

"Swimming? Really?"

"Yeah, since we're right on the ocean, everyone has to learn to swim around here. Classes start in kindergarten and continue through middle school. It's optional at the high school level."

"What about football? Or baseball? Or basketball?" Lauren asked curiously.

"We have a football team, the Dolphins, and the kids all play recreation league baseball and basketball, but swimming's the big sport around here."

Turning her gaze on Jinx, Lauren asked, "So what do you teach?"

Gesturing around the room at the gorgeous murals, Jinx laughed. "Art, of course."

"*You* painted all of this?" Lauren asked in amazement.

"Well, I didn't care for the starving artist idea, so I decided to become an art teacher. You know what they say — *those who can, do. Those who cannot, teach.*"

"Jinx. You're not giving yourself enough credit. You are very talented. This is amazing."

Jinx grinned. "I knew I was going to like you." "Listen, I've got a meeting at the county office in a bit. How about I stop back by on the way to lunch and pick you up? Everyone will be together at lunch and I can introduce you."

Chapter Five: We Never Order Sea-food

Jinx drove Lauren to an adorable hole-in-the-wall restaurant called the Beach Bum. "Just so you know, the restaurant choice is for your benefit. We usually pick something closer to school, and we *never* pick seafood," Jinx said.

Lauren laughed. She could appreciate how living near the beach could ruin your taste for seafood.

"This place has the best fried oyster basket in town," Jinx continued. "They do a great blackened grouper at dinner, and in the late spring, the she-crab soup is to die for."

"So, you *never* order seafood?" Lauren asked, laughing at Jinx's clear enthusiasm for the subject.

"Well, maybe I still sneak some when the others aren't looking."

Lunch was a madhouse of introductions and stories of summer adventures. Most of the elementary school teachers were young and married and had children at Oceanside or in the Little Fishes Daycare nearby. All of them seemed quite grateful that school was starting back. Apparently, a summer of entertaining small children made the upcoming ten-hour workdays very appealing. Jinx, Anne, and Lauren were the only single women at the table. Lauren guessed she and Jinx were about the same age. Anne, with a long gray braid down her back, was clearly much older than the others. Lauren made a mental note to ask Jinx about Anne's story later.

Lauren's fried oysters were, as promised, delicious. She

had always loved the beach and enjoyed seafood. Beach camping had been a favorite family activity before her parents' death. As a child, she had walked past the permanent trailers at the campground and fantasized about what it would be like to live at the beach. When she had seen the Oceanside Elementary banner at the education job fair, she had made a beeline for it. She had, of course, applied to other schools, but her heart had been set on Oceanside.

Lauren attempted to hide a yawn while one of the young married teachers, Gina maybe, told a hilarious story about forgetting to change her toddler into a swim diaper at the pool. She wasn't bored, but between moving and the adrenaline rush of starting a new job, she was exhausted.

She had spent the last two days unpacking and setting up her new house. Well, it wasn't exactly a new house. Her new home was about fifty years old. Thanks to the sale of her condo, she had been able to put a massive down payment on the quaint older home on the beach. Daniel Alonzo had been concerned about the age of the home and had insisted she have it carefully inspected. When the inspector had assured Daniel that although the home was old and could use some updating, it was sound, Lauren had made an offer that afternoon.

Jinx nudged her shoulder. "Hey, you look beat. Are you ready to head back to school?"

Lauren was embarrassed to be caught in a yawn but nodded. "Sorry, I just moved in, and I'm still unpacking."

"Don't worry about it. I crashed every afternoon for months when I started teaching."

As Jinx motioned for the waiter to start bringing the bills, one of the women suggested that they have a girls' night out to show Lauren around. Lauren smiled gratefully. "That would be amazing. I would love that."

On the way out the door, Jinx whispered, "I think she really just wants another night away from her kids. Her two boys are obnoxious, and her husband's useless."

"Oh God, please tell me they're not in first grade."

Lauren sympathetically laughed when Jinx responded, "No, but they do take art."

Back at school, Lauren was concerned when Elouise flagged her down as she entered the building. "You need to go see Mister Melbourne immediately." Lauren considered asking Elouise what he wanted but decided against it.

Being called to the principal's office was just as intimidating as an adult as it was as a kid. Something about being summoned inspired guilt. As she walked to his office and stopped in front of his open door, Lauren braced herself. She had only been here a few hours — what could she possibly have done wrong?

Mr. Melbourne sat behind a dark wooden desk that looked too large for the room. A few taped cardboard boxes sat near the door. Motioning Lauren into the room, Melbourne moved the stack of framed pictures and diplomas that filled the only remaining chair. "Sorry for the mess," the older man began.

"No worries, my place looks just like this right now." *God, that was stupid. Why did I say that?*

Laughing, Mr. Melbourne nodded. "I bet it does. Are you all settled? Do you need anything?"

Lauren forced her shoulders to relax and smiled. "No, sir, I'm good. I just need to finish unpacking and do a little shopping."

"Good to hear. Good to hear. I understand that you have already made some friends?" Melbourne asked, nodding toward the hall.

Lauren was glad she hadn't asked Elouise any questions. Apparently, Elouise had already shared her lunch plans with Mr. Melbourne. She would need to be careful around Elouise.

"Yes, sir, Jinx, I mean Rebecca, took me out to eat and

introduced me to everyone."

"Jinx? Hmph. That one's a hot mess." His words implied a problem, but the smile on his face belied his criticism.

"Stick with her. She'll be a good friend. I think you and she are about the same age," he said, glancing down at a folder open on his desk. "Just try not to let her get you into too much trouble."

"Yes, sir."

"And you can stop calling me sir, as well. In exactly three days, my name will be Dan Melbourne, not sir."

"Yes, sir, ah, yes . . . thank you."

He laughed at her confusion. "Dan will be fine."

"So, I just wanted to go over a few things before school starts. First, I'm sure you've been informed" — Dan cut his eyes slightly to indicate Elouise's desk in the front office — "that I'm retiring."

Interesting, Even Dan Melbourne understands Elouise's place in the pack.

"The new principal, Mister Scott, will unfortunately not be here until the second day of school. I'll stick around long enough to get things rolling, and then he'll take over."

Lauren was bleary eyed by the time Dan had *gone over a few things*. Morning duty, afternoon duty, faculty meetings, subject area meetings, committee meetings, textbook selection, first aid training, open house, registration, lesson plans, state curriculum — the list was endless. On top of all of that, there was the Introduction to the Exceptional Child class that she would need to pick up at the local college. The class was required by the county but hadn't been part of her degree. Dan had assured her that it wasn't a problem. Anyone transferring from outside the county school system would be required to take it as well.

The front office was empty and the halls dark by the time she left the office. The hall lights flickered on automatically as she made her way back to her classroom to retrieve her belongings. Jinx had left her a note scribbled on a piece of primary manuscript paper.

Call me if you need anything. See you tomorrow. Dress comfortably. We will be working in the bookroom. She had added her phone number below a quickly sketched drawing of a shark that looked suspiciously like Elouise.

CHAPTER SIX: TO MY NEW LIFE

Lauren stood in the middle of her new house and sighed. There was too much left to do. While she hadn't brought much from her condo, she had retrieved several boxes that had been in storage since her parents' death. Boxes of memories from her childhood, furniture, pictures, and belongings that had been boxed up for years now stood taunting her in her new old house. Not tonight, she decided, then continued to the kitchen. A glance in the refrigerator reminded her that she needed to go grocery shopping as well. Grabbing a bottle of wine, a red plastic cup, and a box of cheese crackers, Lauren headed for her favorite part of the house. The backyard consisted of a scruffy patch of grass that quickly gave way to sand and sea daisies. A fire pit was surrounded by weather-silvered Adirondack chairs and canopied by branches of ancient live oaks dripping with Spanish moss. Irregular stepping-stones peeked through the sand, leading to a gap in the seagrass-dotted dunes that fenced in her private yard. She could hear the waves crashing as the tide changed a few hundred yards from her house. To the left and right palms, saw palmetto, and assorted scrub screened her from neighbors. She loved this backyard almost more than the house itself. The chairs looked a little rickety, and she might add some flowers for color, but otherwise, it was perfect. She mentally added firewood and matches to her growing shopping list.

Her phone startled her out of her reverie. Glancing at the caller ID, she recognized Nick's number. She let the call go to voicemail, switched the phone to vibrate, and slipped it into a pocket. Striding across her yard, Lauren made her way through the gap and onto the public beach. Finding a nice spot to sit and watch the waves, Lauren burrowed into the sand and poured herself a drink. "To my new life." She toasted herself with a smile. But somewhere in the back of her mind, she thought about Nick's call and amended, "To my new life . . . alone." Halfway through the bottle of wine, Lauren felt her phone vibrate again. *Probably Nick again.* Ignoring the call, she decided to head inside and get some sleep.

As Lauren made her way across the cooling sand, she worried that Nick's calls would haunt her sleep. She knew her strength was in refusing to talk to him. *If*—well, to be honest—*when* she talked to him, he would twist her heart. He would say all the right things, all the things she wanted to hear. *I love you. I miss you, I'm sorry,* and the worst of all, *I need you.* That one always got her—*I need you.* Somehow, he would make her feel that it was her fault that he had cheated on her. He would imply that she was lacking in some way or that she hadn't lived up to his impossible expectations. He would twist everything until she believed that she had truly failed in some manner. She would accept the blame and end up apologizing that he had *needed* to sleep around. God, it sounded so absurd when she thought about it, but she had been down this road with Nick before.

As Lauren climbed the stairs to her master bedroom, she promised herself that she would refuse to answer Nick's calls. *He's three hours away, what can he do?* She could get over him if she could just cut him out of her life. Lauren dropped her sandy clothes on the bathroom floor and rinsed her feet in the giant antique claw tub. Stepping out of the tub, she caught a glimpse of her reflection in the mirror. Her windswept hair fell loose onto her tanned shoulders. Feeling a familiar pang, she slid her thumb across a nipple. It hardened under her touch. Biting her lip, she decided it was time to christen her new bed. Strolling nude from her bathroom, she rolled her nipples between her thumb and index finger. Surprisingly, it was Sawyer, not Nick that she saw when she stretched out on her bed and closed her eyes. Lauren slid her hand between her legs to find that she was already soft and wet. She shivered as she slid a finger across her clitoris. Sex with Sawyer had been mind-blowing. She imagined his face above hers as she worked her fingers between her legs. She felt him sliding into her as her pace quickened. Maybe it was the memory of the sexy stranger or the dangerous adventure of a one-night stand, but it was Sawyer's name, not Nick's, that she cried out as the world exploded around her. She fell asleep thinking that it was such a shame that she would never see the dazzling stranger again. He was back home with her past. It was a catch twenty-two. If she hadn't been leaving, she wouldn't have fucked him, but because she left, she would never see him again. Nicholas Weaver didn't show up in her dreams at all.

CHAPTER SEVEN: CAN YOU KEEP A SECRET?

The following days were a whirlwind. An entire day of pre-service had been spent sorting and delivering textbooks and workbooks. Various committee meetings had been held to discuss curricula. Special education teachers, speech teachers, and all the other extracurricular teachers, including Jinx, had been by to discuss scheduling. Finally, the afternoon of the open house, Elouise had hand delivered her roster of students.

"Here's your list of kiddos," Elouise said as she handed her a printed list of names. "Lucky you, you have the new boss' daughter. I think her name's Molly."

Inside her head, Lauren panicked. *Oh shit. I do not need the principal's kid in my class the first year.* Outwardly though, Lauren smiled at Elouise sweetly. "Fantastic. I can't wait to meet her."

"Aren't you worried that he'll be watching you? That maybe, he'll be harder on you?"

Lauren was, of course, worried about exactly that. But she wasn't going to give Elouise the pleasure of seeing her sweat. "Not at all. I'm sure he just wants whatever's best for his daughter."

Whatever Elouise intended to say next was interrupted when Jinx popped her head into the room and asked, "Hey, do you want to grab an early dinner before the open house starts?"

When Elouise left the room, Jinx burst into laughter. "That was awesome. I heard the whole thing. She set you up. I guarantee she put that kid on your roll purposely. She expected you to freak out, and you didn't. Beautiful. Just beautiful."

"Oh, I'm freaking out. I just wasn't going to let her see it."

"Don't worry about it. We've all had to teach each other's kids at some point. It usually works out fine."

"Usually?" Lauren asked cynically.

"Usually." Jinx laughed.

Oceanside Elementary Open House was a blur of worried parents and little faces. She couldn't remember all of them, but she did remember Molly Scott. Molly's dark curls contrasted startlingly with her blue eyes and pale skin. At six years old, she still had her baby fat, but Lauren could see what a beautiful woman she would become. The woman with her shared the same dark curls, but her eyes were hazel instead. Paula Scott had probably been considered attractive in her time, but she lacked the perfect combination that had come together in Molly. Lauren noticed a few strands of silver in Paula's hair as she bent to greet Molly.

"Hi, Molly," she began. "I'm Miss Mills, and I'm going to be your teacher this year." Molly clung to Paula's hand and tried to slip behind the woman's legs. Noting the girl's reticence, Lauren added, "You know what? I'm new here and I'm kind of scared about it. Since we're both are new, do you think you and I could be friends?"

Molly tilted her face up to Paula and the older woman nodded. "Okay," Molly whispered.

"I tell you what. I am going to bring a very special treat to share with the class on the first day. Do you think you could help me give out my treat?"

The idea of being a helper clearly intrigued the little girl. Peeking from behind Paula a bit, she asked, "What kinda treat?"

"Can you keep a secret?"

"Uh-huh." Molly nodded.

"You can't tell anyone, okay?" Lauren motioned for the little girl to come closer so she could whisper in her ear.

When Lauren finished telling her secret, a grin spread across Molly's face. Paula mouthed *thank you* as Lauren stood back up. In a voice Molly couldn't hear, Paula whispered, "She's not usually this shy. She really misses her daddy." Lauren felt a pang of camaraderie with the little girl. She knew what it was like to miss your parents.

Dan Melbourne had already told her that Mr. Scott would be meeting with the staff on Tuesday afternoon, but to be polite, Lauren asked, "When's Mister Scott going to get here?"

"The sale on the house closes on Monday, so he should be here early next week."

"I'm glad. I look forward to meeting him."

As the two walked away, Lauren placed her index finger in front of her lips and reminded Molly, "Remember, it's a secret. I'll see you on Monday."

The little girl nodded and disappeared into the crowd. *Well, Mrs. Scott seems nice enough and Molly's a little sweetheart. Now, I've got the weekend to figure out how to make the apple cookies I just promised her.*

Jinx turned out to be lifesaver again. In addition to her artistic ability, she was also an excellent cook. She and Lauren spent Saturday afternoon at Jinx's house cutting out and decorating several dozen apple-shaped sugar cookies. When the cookies were safely packed in a box to be transported to school on Monday, Jinx opened a bottle of wine and they moved to her back deck.

"So, tell me about yourself," Jinx began. "I know your name, rank, and serial number. Now tell me the rest."

"Well, there's not much to tell. My mom and dad died in

an accident three months before I graduated from high school. My best friend's parents took me in and kept me out of trouble until I was old enough to live on my own. I worked as a waitress for a couple of years after high school. Eventually, I got it together and went to community college and earned a teaching degree. And so, here I am."

"What about guys? Any boyfriends pining away back home?"

When a slight frown flickered across Lauren's face, Jinx apologized, "Oh damn. I'm sorry. I shouldn't be so nosey."

"No, it's okay," Lauren promised. "Yes, I suppose someone's pining away at home, but I'm not pining for him."

On further thought, Lauren added, "Well, he may be pining away, but I imagine it's from someone else's bed."

"Ouch," Jinx sympathized. Lauren reached for the wine bottle to refill her glass and told Jinx the drama-filled story of Lauren and Nick.

"Jeez, I hope you're really over him this time. He sounds like an asshole."

Lauren immediately felt the familiar desire to defend Nick. She and Dani had had this conversation a million times. There was no lost love between Dani and Nick. Lauren knew that Dani thought he was a jerk and that she should have dumped him a long time ago. Lauren's brain knew this to be true, but her heart generally had a different opinion.

Lauren fought the urge to defend Nick. He was a jerk and an asshole. She needed to move on. He was never going to change. *But I'm going to change.*

"Yeah, he really is an asshole," Lauren announced after an uncomfortably long pause.

Jinx burst out laughing. "It took you a while, but you came out with it." Sobering, she asked, "But are you over him?"

She looked her new friend in the eyes and admitted, "I want to be."

"Well, that's a start," Jinx agreed.

Changing the subject, Lauren sat up straighter in her chair. "What about you? Is there no Mister Jinx waiting in the wings?"

"No, I'm afraid not, and the pickings are pretty slim around here," Jinx proclaimed too enthusiastically. Seeing Lauren's serious face staring at her, she added, "Well, there was once, but not anymore."

"Husband or boyfriend?" Lauren asked.

"Fiancé."

"What happened?"

"He died."

Lauren held her wine glass halfway to her lips. She glanced over to see if Jinx was joking. "Oh, Jinx. Why didn't you tell me to mind my own business?"

Jinx smiled ruefully at Lauren. "Don't worry about it. It was a long time ago, and I'm sure someone would've told you the story eventually. It was big news around here for a while."

Grasping at a straw, Lauren attempted to divert the story. "So, it sounds like you grew up around here?"

"In this very house."

"Seriously?"

"Seriously. I still sleep in my childhood bedroom. I could have moved into the master when my mom finally passed, but it just seemed creepy to sleep in my parents' room." Noticing Lauren's look of confusion, Jinx laughed and added, "Oh don't worry, it's not as *Flowers in the Attic* as it sounds. I knocked out a wall and added a bathroom to make a new master suite downstairs. The construction guy said having a master on the main would be a big selling point someday."

Unsure what to say, Lauren jumped ship again. "I really loved that book."

Jinx laughed. "Remind me never to play you in dodgeball."

Laughing together, they spent the afternoon discussing

favorite books, favorite movies, and favorite bands. Neither woman allowed the conversation to return to relationships. Lauren was sure she would tell Jinx about Sawyer one day, but for now she wanted to hoard the memories for herself. She was just as sure that with enough time and wine, Jinx would tell her about her dead fiancé one day.

The first day of school was exhausting. Two kids had cried when they were dropped off and another had thrown up on the grass carpet, forcing her to give the kids an extra recess while the custodian attempted to save her rug. The criers had eventually calmed down and quite happily enjoyed the rest of the day. Molly had been shy at first, but after Lauren introduced her to a few other girls, she had disappeared into the treehouse loft to play until class started. The puker had been sent home by the nurse with the stomach flu. She surveyed the room, noting all the surfaces that could be harboring cooties. *Great, now we'll all get sick.*

The rest of the day had gone well. Mr. Melbourne — Dan — had told her that all she needed to worry about the first day was to *get them here, get them fed, and get them home.* If she could do that, she would have had a good first day. Based upon that rubric, she decided that it had been a successful day. Who knew teaching first grade was such a workout? She had done her student teaching, so she knew how hard the job was. *But I've got to do it again tomorrow and the next day and the next, for the next one-hundred-seventy-nine days.*

Tuesday came way too early. Lauren stood, staring into her closet. She would meet her new boss today, and she knew it was never too soon to make a good first impression. Her gaze fell on the stark white dress shirt that she had borrowed when she had snuck out of Sawyer's house while he slept. She had justified snatching the shirt by deciding that the pre-dawn air was probably a little chilly. But the truth was, she had put it on when she got up to get a drink of water and enjoyed how the expensive fabric smelled of his cologne. A souvenir? A trophy? She didn't care. She just wanted something to remember the night. Grabbing the white shirt, she added a pair of leggings, a wide belt, and ballet flats, reproducing one of her favorite Audrey Hepburn looks. Feeling confident, she grabbed her keys and headed for school.

The second day of school was almost as drama filled as the first. The same two students cried and clung to their parents' legs. The parents, she decided, were part of the problem. Susan Clayton, one of the weeper's mother, told her that she was returning to the workforce and that it had been a difficult adjustment for little Justin. Watching their interaction, Lauren decided that it was Susan that was probably struggling with her decision, and little Justin was just feeding off her anxiety. Lauren politely suggested that Susan consider dropping Justin off at the front of the school rather than walking him into school. Susan looked annoyed at first, but her features relaxed when Lauren added, "It will be easier for both of you."

Recognizing Lauren's intent, Susan gave her a watery smile. "I suppose this has been pretty hard for me. I've always stayed at home. It's been a big adjustment for us — for me."

"I promise, he'll be fine. If there are any problems, I'll call you."

The other wailing child was placated when a few new friends arrived and coaxed her into the play kitchen. Even the sick student had returned. The doctor had assured his parents that it had just been a case of the nerves. Lauren smiled to herself as the last parent left. At last, she had her entire class to herself. She rang a small hand bell to alert the children that it was time for the morning meeting.

Gathering her little tribe in a circle, Lauren began, "So, does anyone have anything to share this morning?" Every hand in the room went up.

"Molly? What about you? What do you want to share?"

"My daddy will be here today."

Lauren smiled at the happy little girl. "I know. That is very exciting. I know you have been really looking forward to that."

Justin couldn't wait and blurted out, "I got to eat chicken nuggets and a milkshake for dinner last night."

"Justin, you need to raise your hand and wait your turn," Lauren admonished.

"Yes, Miss Mills," Justin droned, dropping his head.

Lauren knew that the boy needed to learn self-control, but she felt bad. It was only the second day of school. Justin's head shot up with a big grin when Lauren added, "I really like chicken nuggets, too."

Lauren threw herself into the morning with enthusiasm but was relieved when Jinx stuck her head in the door and asked aloud, "Who is ready for art class?" With the students lined up in the hallway, Jinx added quietly, "Faculty meeting this afternoon. New boss is finally here."

"Have you seen him yet?"

"No, but he must be something, even Elouise is primping. I caught her putting on lipstick this morning."

When her class returned, Lauren pulled out one of her favorite children's books and gathered them all on the carpet. "Has anyone ever had a really bad day?" she began. The children enthusiastically participated as she read the story.

"Do you think he really moved to Australia?" Justin asked as she closed the book.

"I don't know. What do you think?"

Appearing surprised to have the question turned back on

him, Justin furrowed his brow as he thought about it. "I think things got better the next day. I think he would have missed his mom if he had moved to Australia."

"I think you are probably right. Things do usually get better."

By the time the afternoon dismissal bell rang, Lauren wanted nothing more than to go home and collapse. She dropped into one of the nearby beanbags and sighed.

"Come on. Let's go. I want to get a front-row seat," Jinx announced as she leaned in the door.

"I'm coming. I'm coming." *Why do I always have such impatient friends?*

The media center was packed by the time they made it down the hall. Everyone, it seemed, was eager to meet Mr. Scott. Lauren and Jinx eventually found seats near the back of the crowd. She had turned around to speak to another teacher when she heard a deep familiar voice from the front of the room.

Mr. Melbourne stood at the front of the library beside a tall, dark haired man in a well-cut light linen suit. Lauren didn't even have to hear Dan Melbourne introduce him to know that she was looking at Mr. Scott—Mr. *Sawyer* Scott—her new boss. What was she feeling? A million thoughts flew through her head at once . . . confusion, excitement, pleasure, and finally—fury. Fury, because when she finally connected the dots, she realized that they led straight to Paula Scott, Molly's mother and Sawyer's wife. *The son of a bitch is married!*

As she was working this out in her head, Sawyer Scott had begun to introduce himself to the assembled faculty. "I'm so sorry I couldn't be here for the first day of school. I had to wrap up the final details on my old house. But I'm all yours now." His offer and the dazzling smile had every woman in the room sigh.

"Oh my God," Jinx whispered without turning her head.

"He's gorgeous."

Lauren didn't respond. She was busy trying to disappear into the woodwork. When she got no response, Jinx turned to look at Lauren. "Hey, are you okay? You look like you're going to pass out."

"Shhhhh. I'm fine," Lauren whispered, hoping not to draw any attention.

"What . . ." Jinx began.

Turning to look into Jinx's eyes, she pleaded, "Later. Okay?"

Unfortunately, the conversation had drawn exactly what she didn't want right now, Sawyer's gaze.

Sawyer stopped mid-sentence. Finally finding his voice, he asked, "Are you okay?"

Jinx could clearly see her distress — she responded, "She's fine. She's just not used to the heat yet."

Sawyer nodded. "Yes, it's kind of warm in here."

Sawyer continued his speech, but she didn't hear a word for the blood pounding in her ears. When he finally wrapped up his remarks, Lauren whispered to Jinx, "Get me out of here. Please."

Slipping through the crowd, they managed to escape. Safely in the parking lot, Jinx asked, "You want to tell me what all that was about?"

Lauren nodded. "I will, but not right now. Okay?"

"But you already know him, right?"

Lauren hesitated. "Yes, I already know him. I mean, I met him . . . once." Recovering some of her self-possession, Lauren asked, "Do you think anyone else noticed?"

"Noticed what? That he was struck blind, deaf, and dumb when he saw you?"

Lauren gave her friend a panic-stricken glance. "Really?"

"No. I'm teasing." Jinx laughed. "I only noticed it because I saw your reaction. He actually covered for you pretty well."

"Yeah, he's good at that," Lauren murmured.

"What?"

"Nothing. Never mind. Jinx, I need to go. I promise I'll explain all of this later, but right now I need to go home. I need time to think."

What Lauren really needed was Dani. She had talked to Dani several times since she had moved, but the conversations had been light chit chat about her new house, her new job, and Dani and Matt's wedding plans. She needed her best friend right now.

Lauren was probably halfway home by the time Sawyer made it through the handshakes and introductions after the faculty meeting. He had surreptitiously looked for her in the crowd, but he knew she was gone. His mind was swirling with confusion. *Why? How?* He couldn't even manage a complete, coherent thought.

Paula strolled in with Molly as he glad-handed the last of the faculty. "Daddy!" Molly shouted as she bolted into his arms.

"My Molly! I missed you like crazy," he announced as he lifted her. "How's school?"

"It is awesome. My teacher is Miss Mills, and she is the prettiest lady in the whole world."

"Hey," Paula announced, pretending to be offended. "I thought you said that I was the prettiest lady in the whole world."

"You can be the prettiest auntie in the whole world." Molly giggled.

"Well, okay," Paula agreed.

"I know you're the best sister," Sawyer promised.

"Hey, I'm the only sister you've got."

"Yeah, well. You know what I mean," Sawyer added,

bumping his shoulder against his twin sister's.

"Come on. I'll buy you guys some dinner. So, Miss Molly? Have you made any new friends?"

Molly spent the next hour sharing every detail of the last two days with her father. Finally, after he and Paula managed to get her to stop talking and eat some of her hamburger and fries, they headed home. Home, for the moment, was Paula's house. He was still house hunting. He knew what he wanted. He just hadn't found it yet. While he appreciated Paula's offer to stay with her indefinitely, he wanted to find a new home for Molly. As he carried Molly upstairs to her temporary bedroom, she murmured sleepily, "Daddy?"

"What, pumpkin?"

"Did you make any new friends?"

Molly's eyes were closed before he could whisper, "I don't know. Maybe."

CHAPTER EIGHT: COMFORTABLE SLIPPERS LOVE

Talking to Dani the night before had made Lauren homesick for her best friend. *Maybe this is all a mistake. Maybe I should chuck it all and move back home.* But the truth was that Dani was starting a new life as well. Going back wouldn't solve anything. Dani told her, although she already knew, that she was going to have to move forward. Dani's suggestions of ways to punish Sawyer, while anatomically impossible, had eventually made her laugh.

She had made a mistake. She had slept with a married man. It wasn't the end of the world. After all, he was the one who was cheating. She was just an innocent bystander. Well, maybe not entirely innocent, but he hadn't had a ring on, nor had he mentioned a wife or a daughter. Sweet Molly was the knot in the string. If not for Molly, she would tell Sawyer off in no uncertain terms. But she had Molly to consider. She couldn't . . . wouldn't . . . do anything to hurt that sweet little girl.

The question that Dani had left hanging last night remained unanswered. *Why am I so upset about it?* It was a one-night stand. She hadn't even stayed long enough to get his last name. She had snuck out like a thief in the middle of the night. Spying Sawyer's shirt that she had tossed on the chair the night before, she grimaced. *Actually, just like a thief!*

She hadn't expected to see him again.

Really, this should be funny.

So, why does the thought of him with Paula make my stomach twist in knots?

Attempting to dress for school the next day, Lauren stood naked, staring into her closet. *I'm not dressing for Sawyer — uhm, Mr. Scott. I'm not interested in what that man thinks or does. He's a stranger and I intend to treat him like one.*

Despite her mental commitment to disregard the man, she slipped into what Dani called her *going to get laid* silk panties and bra. Eventually choosing a flowing black maxi dress that accentuated her tanned skin and blonde hair, she took one last glance in the mirror. She was flushed. Her eyes were bright, and her lips were ripe and full without the benefit of any makeup. She looked exactly how she felt, aroused. Even with her conscious mind promising that she wanted nothing to do with the two-timing cheating jerk, her body had moved on to remembering how the rough pad of his thumb had slid across her nipples, how his cock had filled her as he slid into her, how his eyes had glinted dangerously, as she peered through her lashes while she sucked him.

"Well, hell!" she muttered in frustration as she headed for the door.

Elouise, dressed in a brightly flowered dress, flagged Lauren down as she attempted to slip down her hall unnoticed. "Yoo-hoo, Miss Mills. There was a delivery for you first thing this morning."

Lauren stopped. *What in the world?* Following Elouise back to the office, she spied the immense bouquet of red roses perched on the sign-in counter.

"We don't usually accept deliveries like this but . . ." Elouise sniffed. Lauren wasn't sure whether Elouise was annoyed or just nosey. Lauren's mind raced. *Who would have sent me flowers?* The only person she could imagine was Dani, but she wouldn't have sent red roses. Everyone knew red roses meant love. A tiny voice whispered in her head. *Sawyer?*

"Well, don't just stand there. Read the card," Elouise demanded. Lauren jerked back to reality. She hadn't even noticed the discreet white envelope perched among the stems. Pulling the note loose from its plastic pick, she slid a single card from the envelope.

I have changed. Please forgive me. My life is meaningless without you. Come home and marry me. Nick.

Lauren's heart leaped for a moment. Nick wanted to marry her. He loved her and wanted her to come home. She knew she should toss the roses and the card into the nearest dumpster, but she didn't. Her brain was shouting. *Don't fall for this. Don't let him draw you back into his web.* But her heart was hearing wedding bells and imagining family picnics with Dani's and her children playing together while Matt and Nick tossed a football nearby.

"Oh, dear, he sounds wonderful." Elouise sighed, peering over her shoulder. Lauren had forgotten all about Elouise. Startled, she turned to face the older woman.

"Can you just not mention this to anyone for now?" she pleaded.

As if on cue, Sawyer pushed his way through the office door. He took in the tableau — Lauren's flushed face, the roses, and the conspiratorial look on Elouise's face. "Nice flowers," he coolly offered as he continued past to his office. In the charged silence that followed, Lauren heard his office door close. She felt the door clicking shut like a punch.

Lauren tried to concentrate on her students for the rest of the day. Sawyer's entrance at what should have been an exciting and joyous moment had thrown her off balance. She had seen enough romantic comedies to know how this was supposed to go. She should have rushed out the door, throwing all responsibility to the wind. She should have flown on the wings of love home to fall into her true love's arms.

Instead, she calmly carried her flowers to her classroom and prepared to teach first graders how to step-count by threes.

Why am I not rushing home to Nick? This is what I've been waiting for the last four years. Isn't it? Boy meets girl, and they fall in love, boy proposes, girl starts planning the wedding. Isn't that the way it's supposed to go? Boy had proposed, but girl was busy teaching math to six-year-olds. Shouldn't she be excited and happy? Shouldn't she have wanted to rush straight home to Nick?

And then there was Sawyer.

Lauren was waiting impatiently for that other shoe to drop. Surely he would say something today. She wanted him to say something, and at the same time she dreaded it. What could he possibly say? *Is he just going to pretend he doesn't know me? Is he embarrassed about our one-night stand? Does he regret it? Why do I even care?*

Lauren's brain buzzed with questions that had no answers. She was grateful when the bell rang and her charges came tumbling in all noise and chaos. She was thankful that teaching first graders required all her attention. For a few hours, she was able to put aside her personal issues to deal with more important crises, like hair ribbons that had come loose and little shoes that needed re-tying. When the day finally ended and Jinx stuck her head in the door to ask if she wanted to go out to dinner, she jumped at the distraction.

"Where do you want to eat?" Jinx asked as they headed up the hall.

"I don't care really," she announced but added as an afterthought, "somewhere with booze. I really need a drink."

"One of those days, huh?" Jinx laughed.

"You have no idea."

They ate dinner on the outdoor deck that overlooked a marshy inlet of a small family-owned Italian restaurant. With a lacy web of string lights overhead and the soft lapping of the tide moving into the marsh, Lauren felt herself relax.

Leaning back in her chair, Jinx slipped her shoes off and propped her bare feet on the deck railing. "So, you ready to talk about it?"

Lauren considered dissembling but decided that Jinx would see right through her. "Which part?" Lauren asked, sipping her red wine.

"Well, you can start with the ridiculous bouquet of roses in your classroom."

Without taking her gaze from the darkening marsh, Lauren said, "Nick proposed."

To her eternal credit, Jinx just nodded and asked, "And?"

"God, there's just so much to this story, I don't even know where to start."

"Start with your answer. Do you want to marry Nick?"

"Yes. No—Maybe? I don't know. Nick can be a real ass-hole, but we've been together for four years. I just assumed that we would get married someday. I guess I thought that we would work it out."

"I didn't hear you say that you love Nick."

"I do, I guess. Nick's like comfortable slippers—not very exciting but predictable and easy."

"But?"

Lauren glanced over at her perceptive new friend surprised that she recognized there was a *but*.

"But I have started this new life here. I have a house of my own and a career. I'm not sure I want to give that all up."

Jinx looked at Lauren with a doubtful expression that clearly said, "Yeah, right. *That's* what is holding you back."

"What? Is that not a good enough reason?" Lauren asked, defensively.

"A house you have owned for a few weeks and a job that you have barely begun? No. I'm not buying it. What else is holding you back?"

Lauren was quiet for a few minutes lost in her thoughts. *Surely, Sawyer's not the reason that I'm hesitating. That would be . . . absurd? Ridiculous.* How could she possibly be pinning her hopes on a man that she barely knew, slept with once, and who had failed to acknowledge her in any way?

"Well . . ." Lauren began hesitantly, "I guess there is someone else."

"Aha! Now we get to the good stuff." Jinx grinned as she topped off both of their glasses again.

"Right before I left, I met —" Lauren's confession was interrupted by the buzzing of her cell phone. Glancing down, Lauren frowned. "It's Nick." Lauren just stared at the phone as it continued to buzz in her hand.

"Give it here." Lauren looked at her questioningly but handed her the device.

"*Digame?*" Jinx shouted into the phone in a loud, brassy voice.

Lauren could hear Nick's confusion across the table. "Uh, Lauren? May I speak to Lauren Mills?"

"*No se,*" Jinx continued with a big grin.

Nick, like a typical American, when confronted with someone who didn't speak English, spoke slower and louder. "Lau – ren Mills."

"*Lo siento. No habla Ingles.*"

Jinx clicked the end call button and handed it to Lauren. "Now turn it off. You can tell him that you lost your phone. That'll buy you some time."

Lauren stared dumbfounded at her. "What did you say?"

"I just told him I didn't understand because I didn't speak English."

"You're incorrigible."

"Oh, sweetie. That's one of the nicer things I've been called. Now, turn off your phone and finish your story. You left me hanging."

"Well, as I said, I met someone. It was just one night, a fling. Nick and I had broken up, and I was on my way out of town. I was feeling reckless. Dani, my best friend, and I had gone to a club to celebrate our last night together and to hear her fiancé's band play. We were having a good time, dancing and drinking. About the time the second set started, Nick showed up and was his usual manipulative self. I was about to give in when this gorgeous stranger interfered and saved me. Long-story-short, I ended up going home with him and, well, you can imagine the rest."

Jinx smirked. "Only too well."

"I've never done anything like that before. I don't usually go home with perfect strangers. As a matter of fact," Lauren continued with discomfiture, "I've never had a one-night stand before."

"Stop!" Jinx announced, holding her palm facing Lauren. "Never apologize for your choices to me or anyone else. You did what you did. You're the only one that gets to have an opinion about it."

Lauren didn't understand Jinx's vehemence but appreciated the sentiment. "Anyway—" Lauren continued.

"Let me guess. You get to your new house and new job and make an awesome new friend?" Jinx asked gleefully. "And your second day of work, in walks Mister One-Night Stand?"

Lauren choked on her wine and spluttered, "How did you know?"

"I knew there was a weird vibe between you two."

"Plus," Jinx added with a grin. "You already told me that you knew him somehow."

"So? What am I going to do?" Lauren moaned.

"I think," Jinx said with a glint of amusement in her eyes, "the question isn't *what* are you going to do, but *who* are you going to do?"

Lauren's mouth fell open in bemused shock at Jinx's summation of her problem.

"Close your mouth, sweetie. You'll catch flies."

Lauren collapsed onto her bed fully clothed near midnight. She and Jinx had laughed and traded stories until the restaurant owner had politely suggested that they head home. Jinx had still not shared the story of her dead fiancé, but Lauren wasn't going to push. She would tell her eventually. Lauren felt the room spinning under her. She could hear the answering machine's insistent beep, but she chose to ignore it. She knew there were probably a hundred messages from Nick, but she didn't want to listen to them. Her brain felt fuzzy and her nose was running from too much red wine. She fell asleep giggling to herself.

The following morning, Lauren awoke to an insistent pounding. At first, she thought it was the hangover she richly deserved but eventually she realized the pounding wasn't inside her head. She could hear a muffled voice shouting, "Lauren, open up. Come on, sweetie. You're going to be late to work."

"Oh shit!" Lauren's head exploded in pain as she sat straight up in bed. Lauren bolted to the door if only to stop the noise. Jinx stood outside her door with two large coffees and a bottle of aspirin.

Pushing her way in, Jinx announced, "Come on, lazy bones, we're going to be late."

"What? How?" Lauren stumbled.

"You turned off your phone, remember? I figured that if you're like every other millennial, your phone's also your alarm clock. So, I guessed, correctly it seems, that you might oversleep. Now if you hurry, you still have time to take a shower and get dressed."

Lauren reached for the coffee and sighed. "You're a lifesaver.'

"Nah, just an awesome friend."

As Lauren headed for her shower she added over her shoulder, "I was talking to the coffee."

Lauren and Jinx slid through the front doors of the school just as the morning bell rang. Eloise gave them both a stern look as they signed in for the day. "Jinx, you're a terrible influence."

"How do you know it's not her fault?" Jinx asked in mock indignation.

Elouise looked knowingly at Jinx.

"Yeah, okay fine. You're right. It's my fault. I *am* a terrible influence."

Elouise's face softened. "I just worry about you. You need to . . ."

Jinx interrupted, "I know," and then more softly, "I know."

Lauren watched the exchange between the two women with curiosity. There was clearly more going on here, but the shuffle of small children distracted her. "I better scoot. They will be hanging from the rafters if I'm not in the room when they get there."

"Hey," Jinx said, tossing her the bottle of aspirin with a wink, "you're probably going to need those."

Upon reaching her classroom, Lauren gave a sigh of relief. She had made it before the students. Teaching was a respite from her thoughts. She could immerse herself in teaching and not have to think about anything for the rest of the day. Nick's roses mocked her from a bookshelf, reminding her that her escape was only temporary.

Lauren enjoyed the morning despite her lingering headache. Too much red wine always gave her a sinus headache. The children were happy. Her lessons went well. The day outside her classroom was beautiful, and she looked forward to a nice walk on the beach after work.

"Miss Mills, you have a guest in the main office," Elouise

announced when she picked up the classroom phone.

"Who is it?" Lauren asked, although she knew it could only be one person. Who else would show up, at my job unannounced? Nick, of course. Nick wasn't the kind of guy that you ignored. Why couldn't he have just left me alone to think things out? Why did he have to come here?

Lauren snapped her attention back to the telephone when she heard Elouise ask, "What shall I tell him?"

"Tell him to —" Lauren started in annoyance. Taking a breath to calm herself, Lauren said, "Give me a minute and I'll be right there. Thank you."

After locating a teacher's aide to supervise her class, Lauren strode toward the front office. In a voice that was too loud, Nick proclaimed, "Sweetheart. Oh, thank goodness you are all right. I was so worried. I called and called and couldn't reach you. I was terrified something awful had happened to you."

Lauren could see the pink in Elouise's cheeks as she watched Nick's performance. He had clearly already charmed Elouise. He was good at that.

"Nick, what are you doing here?" Lauren demanded.

"Do you see, Miss Gilbert? Do you see how the woman I love treats me?" Nick asked, turning to the older woman for support.

Before Elouise could speak, Lauren grabbed Nick's arm. "Can we talk outside . . . please?"

Tossing one last long-suffering glance toward Elouise, Nick opened the office door and ushered her out with a flourish. Lauren led him through the big glass doors that fronted the school to the covered portico where the children lined up to be picked up by a car in the afternoon. When they were out of earshot of the school, Lauren rounded on him. "Why are you here?"

"I was worried about you."

"Bullshit," she said a little too loudly. Glancing around, she added more quietly, "You're just ticked that I didn't come running home to you. "Nick, this is my job. You can't just show up here. You have to leave."

"I missed a day of work and drove three hours to see you. I'm not going to just turn around and go home."

"I cannot do this now, Nick. I have a classroom full of kids that are waiting for story time."

"Can't someone else tell them a story? Come on. Get someone to cover for you and we will go somewhere and talk."

Lauren knew him well enough to realize that by 'talk he meant *fuck*. He would say all the right things and they would end up in bed. He would promise her anything she wanted. He would swear that she was the only woman for him. He might even tear up when he talked about living without her. Then they would have sex and he would fall asleep with a self-satisfied grin and she would lie staring at the ceiling wondering if, this time, it really would be different.

"No. I cannot get anyone to cover for me. Please, can we just do this later?"

"And just what am I supposed to do all day?"

Lauren should have seen that coming. He had known that his timing was inconvenient. He had done it on purpose. Once again, she was the bad guy. Too late now. She had already stepped into his snare. "Look" — Lauren sighed, pulling her keys from her skirt pocket — "take my keys and go to my house. The address is on the tag. Wait there. I'll be home as soon as school dismisses. Okay?"

Leaning in close to her, he lifted her chin with his knuckles. "I really do love you, you know?"

Sighing in surrender, Lauren placed her palm against Nick's stomach and nodded. "I know."

Dropping a chaste kiss on her forehead, Nick spun her

keyring on his finger and headed toward his waiting car. He casually tossed over his shoulder. "See you at home."

Lauren breathed out a sigh of relief at his departing silhouette. Problem solved, at least temporarily. Turning back toward the school, Lauren noticed a second departing silhouette, Sawyer. *How much did he hear? How long had he been standing there? Had Nick realized he was there?* Stupid question. Of course, he had. Nick had played her. Again.

Chapter Nine: Sad and Messy

B ack in his office, Sawyer tried to focus on the budget sheets in front of him. He had work to do. He couldn't let his mind wander to beautiful, sensual Lauren Mills. Sawyer had done his best to avoid her. That didn't stop his body from responding to her. Every time her name crossed his mind, his pants grew uncomfortably tight. During the day, he could submerge himself in his work. Running a school required a great deal of attention. At night, though, there was no escape. Every time he closed his eyes, he saw her on her knees with his cock deep in her throat. He could feel her nipples, hard and erect, sliding across his stomach as she trailed hot kisses from his dick to his mouth. Her cries and groans echoed in his mind relentlessly, driving him to lock his bedroom door and ease his desire. Closing his eyes, he tried to imagine that it was her hand sliding up and down his aching cock and that any minute she would ease herself onto him, allowing him entry into her hot wet softness.

It wasn't the same.

He came with her name on his lips and her face in his thoughts, but it wasn't the same — not even vaguely the same. Despite feeling some physical relief, he wasn't satisfied. He felt let down and disappointed. Touching himself and thinking of her was just sad — sad and messy.

He knew he needed to do something. He couldn't go on like this. He was like a horny teenager with a twenty-four/ seven hard-on. He wanted to talk to her . . .to ask her out . . .to fuck her again. But what was the point? *The boyfriend's clearly back in the picture. And what about the fact that I'm her boss?* He was certain that there were rules about fraternization. *And why has she not talked to me?* She seemed as eager to avoid him as he was to avoid her. She didn't even make eye contact with him when they passed in the halls. *Does she regret our night together? Is she embarrassed? Sorry?*

Sawyer tossed the budget papers on his desk and stood abruptly. "Time for action," he announced aloud to his empty office. One way or another he had to ask the questions. Then he had to find a way to live with the answers.

Sawyer was standing in Lauren's classroom doorway when Molly squealed, "Daddy!" He grabbed his daughter as she ran toward him and swung her in the air.

"Hey, how's my little pumpkin?" Molly's exuberant recitation dimmed to a low buzz as Lauren's gaze met his.

Sawyer felt Molly's small hand on his cheek. "Daddy? Daddy? Did you hear what I said? I can count all the way to one hundred and—"

Sawyer interrupted his daughter, "That's amazing, sweetie. You can show me tonight, okay? But right now, I need to talk to your teacher."

As Lauren crossed the room, he took the opportunity to study her. She was even more breathtaking than he remembered. Her blonde hair was pulled back into a low ponytail that draped over one shoulder. She moved with the unknowing grace of a predator, and he was her helpless prey. He felt his heart pounding in preparation for the chase.

"Miss Mills, my daddy needs to talk to you," Molly announced from across the room, as if Lauren hadn't noticed him. She couldn't help but notice him. He filled the room. She remembered the sensation she had felt before—of there just being so much of him. Lauren felt her face warm as she strode across the room toward him. This was the closest she had been to him since that night.

"We need to talk," he began.

Lauren's head spun with all the things that she wanted to say to him. She wanted to tell him that she hadn't stopped thinking about him since that night. She wanted to tell him that her memory of their night played over and over like a song that was stuck in her head. The overwhelming nearness of him made her want to lean into him and smell his masculinity and feel his hard body against hers. She wanted to lift her head and have him lower his lips to hers.

Glancing back at Molly to steel herself, Lauren took a deep breath. She needed to make him understand that she would not pursue a relationship with him now that she knew he was married.

"What can I do for you, Mister Scott?"

Sawyer cleared his throat. "I think it is time you and I had a talk about—"

"I know what you want to talk about," she interrupted, "but I'm not sure what there is to say."

"What do you mean?"

"I mean that I understand the situation now. You have a . . ." She faltered. She couldn't bear to say *wife* and so she substituted, "You have a daughter. That night was . . ."

What? Amazing? Hot? The most exquisite night I ever had?

"That night was a mistake. One that cannot be repeated. Now, if you don't mind, I have a class waiting for snack time."

Closing the door, Lauren felt the prick of hot tears behind her eyelids. She knew it was the right thing—the only thing to do—but it was also the hardest thing to do. She had to find a way to accept the fact that he was married and forget him. A hard break, she knew, was the only way to do it. *Now, if I can only be this strong with Nick.*

CHAPTER TEN: YOU'LL KNOW IT WHEN YOU SEE IT

Sawyer felt as if a cold blade had been forced between his ribs as she closed the door in his face. He had wanted answers. Well, he had them, and now he was going to have to live with them. What had he expected anyway?

Returning to his office, he informed Elouise that he had an appointment to look at a house and wouldn't be back for the rest of the day. This wasn't entirely true. He didn't have an appointment, but having used the excuse, he decided that house hunting might distract him. It was high time that he found Molly a permanent home.

"So, Mister Scott, what is it you are looking for?" Jules Jameson asked stridently. Jules was the epitome of a real estate agent. She was too much everything. The white blouse she wore exploded from her pink jacket in an elaborate drooping bow. Her hair was teased and set in a permanent blonde helmet that no amount of sea breeze could dislodge. The combination of too much perfume and too much hairspray preceded her by a dozen feet. Her makeup, while too elaborate for Sawyer's taste, did a good job of disguising her age. When she sat down at the coffee shop, Sawyer could see the wrinkles and crow's feet she was fighting to hide. She was older than he had initially guessed, maybe sixty. But she had a twinkle in her eye and he had quickly discovered a wicked sense of humor.

"I don't really know how to describe it. I guess I'll know it when I see it?" he offered helplessly.

Hefting a large photo album from her bag and motioning to the waitress for coffee, Jules smiled and declared, "Looks like we've got our work cut out for us then, hmmm?"

An hour later, Sawyer and Jules had defined the broad strokes of what he was looking for—an older home with at least three bedrooms, maybe a cottage style, near the beach would be nice but not a deal breaker, a yard for Molly, and a safe street. He couldn't put an image to the house he wanted. It was more of an idea than a place. It was in his heart, not his head.

"Let's go over to West Beachside and look at a few places. Afterward, there is a wonderful crab shack on the marsh side. I'll buy you lunch," Jules offered as she gathered her purse and hoisted her bag onto her shoulder.

Sawyer pulled the heavy bag from her shoulder. "Here, let me help you with that."

"Hmmm, a gentleman and a looker," Jules teased. "If I was a few years younger . . ."

Sawyer, embarrassed by her blatant flirtation, deflected by announcing, "Why, Miss Jameson, I don't know what you mean. You can't be a day over twenty-five."

"A good liar, too." Jules grinned.

A few houses later, Jules and Sawyer collapsed into a booth in a cool corner of *Jumbo's Crabs*.

Reaching for her iced tea, Jules sighed. "Well, at least we have identified some things you don't want."

"I'm sorry. I hope I haven't wasted too much of your time."

"Sweetie. I've spent the entire day with a handsome young man. How can anyone call that a waste? Don't give up. What you want is out there. I'm sure of it. You just need to keep your eyes open. Like you said, *you'll know it when you see it.*"

As the delicately battered fried spider crab appetizer was

placed on the table before them, Jules leaned in, linking her fingers under her chin. "So, my handsome gentleman, what's your story?"

Earlier in the day, Sawyer would have been taken aback by her bluntness. But after spending the morning with her, Sawyer had become desensitized to her forthrightness. Jules' personality, like everything about her, was over the top. She said exactly what she meant and didn't hesitate. He glanced over the top of his glass to see her waiting with a mischievous glint in her eyes.

"Do you ever *not* say what's on your mind?" he teased.

"Sweetie. If you don't tell people what's on your mind, how will they ever know? Now, quit stalling. Surely there's a beautiful Misses Sawyer Scott that will break my heart."

"There was," he began. "Her name was Anna. She was beautiful and funny and had a smile that could stop time. We had been married for three years when she got pregnant with Molly. The doctors didn't see it coming. It was a fluke. Molly's birth was normal. Then Anna started hemorrhaging and they couldn't stop it. She died without ever seeing our daughter."

Sawyer braced for the sympathetic coos that typically followed his sob story, but Jules just looked at him and smiled. "There's someone else out there for you. I'm certain of it. Just like your house, you'll know it when you find it."

"I don't know if I'm ready for someone else," Sawyer confessed.

Placing her liver spotted hand over his, she sighed. "You will be, sweetie. You will be."

The waitress broke the spell when she dropped the check on the table and asked, "Can I get you some to go cups for your drinks?"

"Gracious, no. Those foam cups make my teeth hurt."

Sawyer reached for the bill, but Jules swatted his hand away. "My treat."

"Jules, please, a gentleman always pays."

Jules smiled coyly and handed him the bill. "Well, hand-some, when you put it that way."

Chapter Eleven: Make Sure You Remember His Name

Lauren straightened her desk for the third time. Noticing a bookshelf across the room, Lauren strode across the room to re-shelve the books so that they were all facing the same way. *Pillows, the apple pillows need straightening.* All real and fabricated projects complete, Lauren stood in the middle of her classroom and looked around. She was almost desperate to find something else that needed to be done. She knew she was stalling. She didn't want to go home and deal with Nick. She was certain that she intended to send him packing but there was still enough doubt in her mind to make her dread the evening.

On the way home, Lauren dusted off an old coping mechanism she called *What I Know*. When her parents had died, Lauren was barely more than a child. Suddenly, she had found herself alone and forced to make adult decisions. When faced with a difficult decision, Lauren would talk herself through it aloud. The process had eventually evolved into her own little form of psychotherapy.

"What I know . . ." she began.

"I know that I don't trust Nick. He's cheated on me over and over.

"I know that we have a history. We've been together forever. Do I still love him? Maybe. Can you just stop loving someone?

"I know that I want — *wanted?* — to marry Nick and live happily ever after.

"I know that if I let him, Nick will smooth talk me right back into his bed. Isn't that what I should want? If I love him, shouldn't I want him to win me over?

"I know that I like my new life here. I like my job. It feels like I'm finally moving forward."

At this point, Lauren paused. Thoughts of her job and her new life lead in a straight line to thoughts of Sawyer Scott.

"I know Sawyer's a married man. There's no future there. I know I cannot let Sawyer influence my decisions."

As usually happened in her personal therapy sessions, Lauren had worked her way to a truth. Sawyer Scott *was* influencing her decisions. Despite knowing that he was unavailable, he was a stumbling block that she couldn't move past.

"I know . . ." she confessed to herself sadly, "I know I wish things were different."

Lauren spent the remainder of her ride home pondering how she should deal with Nick.

Like any good narcissist, Nick was prepared to shower her with love. He had more roses and her favorite wine. He had cooked dinner and lit candles. He had eyes only for her. She knew his apology by heart. He would tell her that she was the most beautiful woman, the only woman that he could ever truly love, that he couldn't live without her.

But Lauren had seen this show before.

"Nick, we need to talk."

"Baby, I know what you're going to say but I've changed. When you left me, you broke me. I realized how empty my life was without you."

Lauren almost laughed at the corniness of his lines. "Nick, your life has never been empty without me — neither has your bed, for that matter."

"You cannot just shut me out, Lauren. Are you really going to throw away our lives together? Our past? All that we've meant to each other? Think of the plans that we had, buying a little house and having a kid or two. Remember how you and Dani planned to raise your children together?"

Nick slipped behind Lauren and wrapped his arms around her. As he trailed kisses down her neck, he whispered into her hair, "Come on, baby. You know I love you. Give me another chance."

Lauren could feel his erection pressing into her ass. Despite herself, she was aroused. Nick was familiar ground. They knew each other inside and out. Slowly, Nick dragged his fingertips along her arms leaving ripples of pleasure. After reaching her forearms, he moved a hand to her breast and slid his index finger across her tightening nipples. *God, not the day for a thin lacy bra.*

As she gave in to the feelings, Lauren's head fell back against Nick's shoulder. He began to work the buttons of her blouse loose. When at last her blouse fell open, Lauren shivered as the cool air touched her hot skin.

"Oh, baby, I've never wanted you more. Can't you feel what you do to me?"

Lauren opened her mouth to say his name as he slid a breast free of her bra and tugged on a nipple, leaving her breathless.

"Tell me," he whispered. It was an old game. "Tell me how bad you want it. Tell me you want me to fuck you."

Leaving her breast, Nick slid his hand down her taut stomach and beneath the waistband of her jeans. Working his way down, she knew he would find her already wet and soft.

"See, baby. See how wet you are for me? Tell me. Tell me you want me. I know you do."

Lauren arched as he slid his finger against her swollen clitoris. All rational thought was gone.

Turning her to face him, he unbuttoned her jeans and slid them to her ankles. She stepped out of them and kicked them away. Kneeling before her, he slid her lacy panties to the side and pushed her legs apart. Sliding his fingers through her hot damp folds, he asked, "Is this what you want? Just say it, baby."

"Yes," she panted. "Yes, damn it!"

Lauren's legs began to quiver as Nick worked his tongue on her clit. The hummingbird tempo of his efforts was pushing her toward the brink.

"Oh God! Oh God, Sawyer! I'm about to come!" Lauren cried.

Nick froze in mid flick.

Lauren opened her eyes, startled that he'd stopped when she was so close. Looking down at the baffled and hurt expression in his dark eyes, she began, "What's—"

"Don't," Nick barked. "Just don't."

Rising to his feet, Nick spit out, "You're a real bitch."

Tears filmed her eyes as she whispered, "Why? What did I do?"

Nick wasn't listening. He was stalking furiously around her living room. Snatching his overnight bag from the hall and his keys from the countertop, he stormed toward her front door. As he wrenched open the door he turned and sneered, "Next time you fuck a guy, make sure you remember his name."

Lauren stood half naked in her living room staring at the door Nick had just slammed behind him. Her body flushed hot and cold as realization dawned. Lauren tensed expecting tears of embarrassment or remorse. But no tears fell. Surprisingly, she began to laugh. She would cry for Nick eventually she knew, but right now, the whole thing was damn funny. She had never seen a more shocked look in her whole life. His expression was priceless.

She knew in her head that what she had done, however unintentional, was horrible. *But honestly, he's put me through worse so many times. Don't I deserve a little payback?* The indignation she felt gave her a powerful feeling of righteous vindication. She relished the idea of having won, for once.

Lauren debated finishing what Nick had started but she knew that if she came now, she would cry. She would lose this powerful feeling, and for now, she wanted to hold on to her small victory. So she did what she had done at every major and minor milestone of her life — she called Dani.

"Dani. You won't believe what just happened," she exclaimed as her friend answered the phone.

When she managed to stop laughing, Dani agreed, "The asshole had it coming. How are you feeling?"

"I feel okay, I think."

Dani stayed quiet and waited while Lauren worked through her feelings as she talked.

"It pissed me off when he showed up at school. I just looked at him and thought, *he doesn't have a clue what I want from life. He just knows what he wants and everyone else will always come second.* I think I'm tired of coming second."

"Good for you. I'm so glad. You deserve better. You always did."

"Now," Dani continued, turning the conversation, "let's talk about the delectable Sawyer Scott."

"Dans, I told you. He's married. He has a daughter."

"Couldn't you just fuck him occasionally, you know, to keep in practice?" Dani teased.

"You know I can't do that. Besides, his daughter's in my class. It would be too weird. I just don't—"

Dani interrupted with a laugh. "Okay, okay. I knew that's what you would say. I was only teasing."

"I wish I could. I really, really, *really* wish I could, but you know I'm a hopeless romantic." Lauren had always had trouble separating sex and love and had fallen for every man she had ever slept with. She'd had her heart broken a few times before she realized that sex and love weren't the same thing to men.

After a moment Lauren added in a less light-hearted tone, "It would never be enough."

"I know, sweetie. I know."

Chapter Twelve: Why Don't We Get Drunk?

Sawyer drove Jules Jameson back to her car at the coffee house and debated returning to work. He really should go back to school. The students had long since been dismissed, but he had plenty of work on his desk. He turned his car toward the school, but in a small rebellion against his crappy morning, he drove past the entrance. He wasn't sure where he was going. He just knew he wasn't going back to work and he wasn't ready to go home. Molly was fine. Paula picked her up in the afternoons because Sawyer generally worked for a few hours after dismissal.

Sawyer rolled down his window and reached to turn on the radio. Jimmy Buffett's *Why Don't We Get Drunk?* blared from the speakers. Normally, he appreciated the song's fun nonchalance but today beach music just reminded him of Lauren. *Why can't I get her out of my mind?* She had made it quite clear that she wasn't interested this morning. As he drove, his mind wandered. He saw those eyes peeking up at him. He could feel the warmth of her smooth skin against his. He could feel the fragile strength in her limbs as he turned her and lowered her to the bed below him. And, my God, he could remember exactly what it felt like when he hovered over her and slid his cock into her for the first time. Tight and hot and so soft, excruciatingly soft. Sawyer shook his head to clear his thoughts when he realized that, once again, thoughts of her had left him painfully aroused. He knew that he needed to get himself under control.

Spotting a sign for a beach access, Sawyer whipped his car into the parking lot. Ditching his tie and shoes on the passenger seat of his car, Sawyer took off across the dunes toward the flat expanse of beach. Reaching the surf, he allowed the cool ocean water to lap over his feet. He stood for a long time allowing the wavelets to reach his bare ankles and retreat pulling the sand from under his feet. Staring out at the horizon, Sawyer felt his earlier tension easing. The ocean had always been a balm to him. He had been thrilled when the position at Oceanside Elementary had come open. He had always wanted to live near the water. The convenience of having his sister, Paula, nearby to help with Molly had made it seem like destiny.

Feeling his breathing slow to match the ebb and flow of the waves, Sawyer began to walk. He loved the feel of the hard-packed sand under his feet. He loved the smell of the salty air and coconut oil from the sunbathers. He caught a whiff of a charcoal fire with hamburgers dripping fat. Sawyer wasn't aware of how far or long he had walked until he looked up and realized that he was no longer on the public beach. The private beaches weren't neatly swept like the public ones. Driftwood and other marine detritus littered his path. Instead of saltwater taffy and ice cream parlors, this part of the beach was backed with homes. Sawyer turned his attention from the ocean to the homes he was passing. Many of them were modern beach houses. To Sawyer, they looked like candy colored spiders with their stilt legs and three hundred-sixty-degree porches perching on the tops of the dunes.

As he continued down the beach, the neighborhood grew a little older and a little shabbier. These houses were built further back from the beach, safely behind the dunes. The houses were still elevated, but in a more graceful way. Beautiful flowers and shrubs fronted elegant old porches filled with rocking chairs and porch swings. The landscaping was more natural. There were no forced patches of green sod here. Native plants dotted sandy yards, and paths were marked by a lifetimes' collection of conch shells. Sawyer felt a smile spreading across his face. This was what he had been looking for. This neighborhood was exactly right. Now he just needed to figure out where, exactly, he was.

The light was fading when Sawyer finally made it back to his car. As he dusted the sand from his bare feet and slid into his stuffy hot sedan, he considered that a new car might be in order as well. Maybe something more suited to the climate, like a jeep or a convertible. He could imagine himself in a nice Mercedes convertible or maybe, an old Jaguar. *No, a green Audi tt convertible with leather seats.* But when he closed his eyes to imagine it, ash blonde hair and big blue eyes smiled back at him from the passenger seat. A polite ding from his cell phone saved him from another frustrating fantasy. He saw he had a text from his sister.

You missed dinner. You might want to grab something on the way home. Are you okay? I called and Elouise said you had left early. By the way, we're out of milk. Can you stop and get some on your way home? Oh, and some conditioner?

Sorry about dinner. I'll go through a drive thru. I went house hunting and found a promising neighborhood. What is conditioner? I'm a guy. Guys don't know these things.

He did, in fact, know what conditioner was. He had been raising Molly alone for the past six years. He knew way more about powders, creams, and lotions than any heterosexual man should know. He adored Molly and had relished every moment of raising her, but he was worried that as she got older, he would be in water over his head. Yet another reason he was grateful that Paula would be around.

Sawyer made a beeline for the milk when he entered the market. As a single father, he had learned to shop efficiently. *You get in, get what you need, get out and pray that the baby sleeps through all of it.* As he grabbed a bottle of baby-safe conditioner and continued toward the front register, the condom display caught his eye. In a spurt of optimism, he grabbed a box and tossed it in his basket.

Lauren didn't sleep well that night. As the adrenaline of her unintentional victory wore off, she began to doubt herself. *Have I just thrown away a sure thing for an impossible fantasy? Sawyer's a fantasy. Nick's a lot of things — a cheating asshole being one — but he's also the man I have loved for four years. He's the man I had planned a life with. Can I fix this? Should I fix this? Is there any way I could be with Sawyer? Could I really do that?*

As the night hours passed and the same questions spun in her head, Lauren decided a hundred times what she would do in the morning, but every decision left her unsettled and unhappy. There simply wasn't a right answer. The only tenable solution was to do nothing. Nick was gone and Sawyer was unavailable. If she just left things as they were, everyone was equally unhappy. *Quite a fairytale. And everyone lived unhappily ever after . . .*

Eventually, she gave up on sleep and wandered outside to the beach. An overripe moon hung over the calmed ocean. The waves had reached the high tide line and were beginning to slip slowly back toward the dark vastness of the ocean. Finding a dry spot to sit above the wrack line, Lauren stared out at the ocean. She loved this place. This was the first home she had ever chosen on her own. She loved her job. She loved her students. Letting Nick go was the right thing to do. She knew that. She had known it before. She had just never had the strength to do it. But fate had intervened and nudged her in the right direction. Now she had to keep moving forward. No looking back. No second thoughts. It stung, but in a way, the decision was liberating. She felt a lightness that made her giddy. On impulse, she slipped her gown over her head and walked toward the waves. She had never so much as skinny-dipped before, but this felt amazing. For the first time in her life, she didn't look to make sure no one was watching. She didn't worry about making a mistake. She strode confidently, gracefully across the moonlit beach. As she eased into the cool water, she felt her body respond with delicious ripples. She felt herself stirring and slid her hand between her thighs. With the dark waves pushing and pulling against her body and the cool night breeze alternately caressing and puckering her nipples, she came in an earth-shattering orgasm that ebbed and flowed through her like hot waves of magma. She cried out into the waves and wind with an abandon she had never experienced before. She was free in a way that she had never been before. She was free and every moment from this moment was a new beginning.

"Uhm, brother dear?" Paula called from the kitchen. "Could you please come and take this upstairs?"

Sawyer looked up from the book he was reading Molly, confused until he recognized the market bag that Paula held in mock disgust between two fingers. Sheepishly, Sawyer slipped Molly out of his lap and snatched the bag from his sister.

"Sorry about that."

When he returned to the living room, Paula held a finger to her lips and pointed to Molly asleep on the couch. "Leave her for now. You can carry her up in a bit. Let's go out on the deck. I suspect there's something you need to tell your big sister."

"You're not my big sister. You're my twin sister."

"Who was born one minute and six seconds before you," she teased.

"Fine. That just means you're one minute and six seconds older."

This was an old shtick between them. Since childhood, she had tried to boss him around claiming she was older. Eventually Sawyer had found her Achilles heel by pointing out that if she was born first that meant she would also be old first.

"Enough, funny boy. Spill. Who is she?"

"Who?"

He knew this was a useless ploy, but he was stalling, deciding exactly what to tell his sister. After a withering look from Paula, he decided he might as well tell her the whole story.

"Okay, Sis, I met this woman . . . at a bar. I know that sounds awful but it's really not as sleazy as it sounds."

Thinking through the next part of the story he amended, "Well on second thought, it really is as bad as it sounds."

"We ended up going home together and well, you know . . ."

"I think I get that part. You can fast forward past the sordid details." Paula smirked.

"Fine, fine. Anyway, she snuck out in the middle of the night. Filched one of my good dress shirts as well. I figured *I'm on my way out of town and I'll never see her again,* so I chalked it up to experience."

"But?"

"But I show up to work at Oceanside and there she sits, wearing my fucking shirt, no less."

"Oh my God. You're kidding, right?"

"No. And get this, she's Molly's teacher. Could it get any more awkward?"

"You mean Lauren Mills? Oh, Sawyer, you've got good taste. So? What did you do?"

"Well for about a week, we just avoided each other. When I finally decided to go talk to her, she wants nothing to do with me and I have no idea why.

"I mean she was all over me that night—" Sawyer added defensively.

"Okay," Paula insisted, holding up her hand, "too much information, bro. I do have to eat again."

"Ha, ha, my point is we had a good time, so I have no idea why she's so standoffish now."

"Maybe she's embarrassed? Maybe she's pissed that it took you so long to talk to her?"

Laughing and stabbing a finger at Sawyer, Paula suggested, "Or maybe, little brother, she was hugely disappointed with what she saw and is just trying to spare your feelings."

"She wasn't disappointed. She was quite satisfied. Multiple times."

"Okay, ick. I know, I set myself up for that one. The important question, Sawyer, is what are you going to do about it?"

"What can I do? She said, and I quote, *we have nothing to discuss.* I mean that's pretty clear. If she was trying to spare my feelings, she failed. But the problem is, Sis, I can't stop thinking about her. I'm like a horny teenager with his first dirty magazine."

"Again, ick. And from now on you wash your own sheets," Paula interrupted.

Chagrined, Sawyer added, "Sorry, but I don't know what to do."

"Well, obviously, you have to find out what the problem is, and then you have to fix it."

In mock sarcasm, Sawyer said, "Oh, great. Thanks, Sis. I'll

get right on that,"

"Glad I could help. Now, that I've solved all your problems, I've got some paperwork to complete from work, so I'm going to say goodnight." As she reached the patio door, she turned and said softly, "You're a great guy, Sawyer. She'll come around. Just hang in there."

CHAPTER THIRTEEN: TO HELL WITH THE PLAN

Lauren was pleased to discover that her euphoria had lasted through the night. She woke up happy and ready to face the world. Realizing that she could dress down for in-service and still feeling a little of her new-found confidence, she chose Sawyer's white shirt and a pair of form fitting dark jeans for school. The outfit made her look sexy, and more importantly, it made her *feel* sexy. In her sexual liberation, she chose to forgo panties and a bra completely. She felt positively decadent. Her body still felt the salt and sand burns from the previous night. Just the memory of it made her draw in a soft breath.

"Excuse me, Miss, have you seen my friend, Lauren Mills?" Jinx asked coyly as she leaned into her classroom to say good morning. "You look fabulous. What in the world has got into you?"

"Well, for starters . . ." Lauren quickly moved to the offending roses and tilted them into a nearby garbage can.

Jinx clapped approvingly. "So, you ditched the cheating bastard?"

"Yep, and you're not going to believe how it happened."

Pulling the classroom door shut behind her, Jinx said excitedly, "Okay, tell me all the dirty little details."

Before Lauren could begin, the intercom interrupted. *Miss Mills, please report to Mister Scott's office.*

"Oh God"—Jinx leered—"maybe he's going to paddle

you."

Lauren had the good grace to blush, but the idea filled her mind with delightful fantasies as she walked toward the office.

"Good morning, Elouise," Lauren chirped. "I believe Mister Scott called for me."

"In his office," she grunted.

Sawyer was neatly dressed in the same low-slung jeans that she had peeled off him just a few weeks ago. A crisp navy button down with the sleeves rolled up showed off his muscular forearms. His eyes, like quicksilver, darkened as he noticed her standing in his doorway. "Come in and please close the door behind you."

Lauren did as she was asked but hovered near the door, insuring an escape route. Seeing her hesitance, Sawyer moved toward her. But for each step he advanced, she took one step back until she found herself with her back against the closed door. Sawyer closed the distance between them. Placing his hand on the door over her head, he leaned in and flicked the collar or his/her white shirt. "I believe this is mine?"

Breathless from his nearness, she managed to squeak out, "Do you want it back?"

This time, it was Sawyer who drew in a shaky breath. "No, you keep it. It looks good on you. But just for the sake of curiosity, why did you take it?"

"I . . . uhm . . . I liked how it smelled. It smelled like you."

"Why did you leave like that? Without even saying goodbye?"

"I don't know. I just got scared, I guess. I couldn't imagine facing you in the morning. I'd never done anything like that before and I knew that I was leaving town, and so I just thought it was the easiest thing to do." She added quietly, "I didn't think I'd ever see you again."

"But now?"

"I don't know, Sawyer. I really don't know."

"What do you want, Lauren?"

In reply she leaned into him and pressed her lips to his gently. "This isn't the plan," her mind screamed. But when she felt him return her kiss her body screamed, "To hell with the plan."

Sawyer moaned as he pressed her against him. She fit perfectly against him, like puzzle pieces meant to click together. Reaching behind her, he twisted the lock on his office door.

"Oh God, Lauren, do you know how you make me feel?"

Looking into his eyes, she smiled and said, "I know how I want to make you feel."

Sawyer felt his knees nearly buckle under him. *Jesus, this woman's going to kill me.*

Reaching to tug *his* shirt from her jeans, he was surprised to find her bare underneath. "Little confident weren't you, Miss Mills?"

She grinned mischievously. "Maybe just a little."

Reaching for him, she tugged at his belt and bent to work loose the button on his jeans. "God bless whoever invented button fly jeans," she mumbled.

Sliding his jeans down far enough to free his cock, she drew her fingernails along its hard length. His dick twitched wildly in response. As she looked up at him through those eyelashes, he saw her bite her lower lip. He watched with rapt attention as she ran her tongue across her upper lip and smiled sweetly. "Is this what you want? Mister Scott? Do you want me to put your cock in my mouth? Do you want me to suck your dick, Sawyer?"

Sawyer was speechless. The first night with her had been spectacular but this new lascivious vixen was beyond his wildest imaginings. All he could do was nod and tilt his pelvis toward her in mute pleading. She slowly drew him in, clearly savoring each inch. When he reached the back of her mouth, she tilted her head so that he could go farther. Reaching up, she grasped his balls and gave a playful squeeze. Sawyer felt himself begin to move against her without conscious thought. *She's so . . .* God help him, he didn't even have the words for it. He felt his world narrowing until all that existed was his dick sliding in and out of her mouth. He knew he should stop. He could feel himself about to lose control. He tried to back up and pull out, but she wrapped one hand behind him and grabbed his ass, pulling him even tighter against her. "Oh, baby, I am about to come," he whimpered. Tilting her head back so that she could see his face, she arched into him and swallowed until he shuddered and stilled.

When he was able to think and see clearly again, he reached down and pulled her from her knees. "I think it's your turn now. Tell me what you want."

Boldly she said, "I want you to lay me across your big old principal's desk and fuck me from behind."

Sawyer could feel himself growing hard again. Briefly he wondered about the people in the office outside his door but then decided that he didn't care. *This is worth my job. Hell, this is worth my life!*

Lauren strolled toward his desk. With her gaze locked on his, she unbuttoned her jeans and slid them down her long legs. Sawyer was surprised to find she was bare under her jeans as well.

As he watched, she slid a finger between her legs and then between her own lips. He pulled her to him, crushing himself against her. He tasted her sweetness as he thrust his tongue between her lips. She tasted like mint toothpaste and sex, an oddly erotic combination. Pulling away from his kisses, she turned and leaned across his desk with her back to him. Looking over her shoulder at him, she whispered, "Please."

Reaching down to the jeans he had managed to finish removing, he fished a condom from the pocket. Lauren grinned.

"Feeling a little confident, were we?"

"Maybe more hopeful than confident."

Sawyer sheathed himself and knelt behind his desk. Her ass, round and perfect, was right in front of him. He reached out and slapped it, not hard but enough to pink the flawless pale skin. He heard her draw in a shuddering breath. Lowering his face to her, he slowly drew his tongue along her most sensitive parts. He felt her quiver below him. "Hold on, baby, we're not even close to done." He slid one finger into his mouth and then into her. He felt her tighten against his finger and he moaned. A second finger joined the first in a slow delicious tempo. With his other hand, he worked her clit, drawing slow figure eights around the sensitive nub.

When he felt her rhythm increase, he slid his fingers from her and stood. His cock ached to be inside her. He didn't think he had ever been this hard in his life. Slowly, he eased into her. His left hand continued its slow dance around her clit. God, she was tighter this way. When he felt her arch against the desk, he abandoned all self-control. He slammed into her over and over until he felt her pulsing below him and surrendered to his need. He came and came. His body shuddered and convulsed with the power if it. When he was finally able to withdraw and clean himself up, he pulled his desk chair over and pulled her onto his lap. She lay against him spent and quiet.

"I didn't really mean for this to happen." Turning her face toward his, he gave her a questioning look. Sighing, she admitted, "Okay, well maybe I did think about it, but you're the one that invited me in here."

"Fine" — he sighed — "I'll take the blame."

"Good," she mumbled against his chest, "then this is all your fault."

"Mhmm," he said drowsily

"What did you want, by the way?"

"I wanted to ask you if you would have dinner with me, Saturday night. Molly and Paula are going to visit cousins up the coast and will be gone until Sunday afternoon."

Lauren's heart ached at the mention of Paula and Molly. She knew she was betraying them, but she was in for a penny, in for a pound now.

"I've got a better idea. Why don't you come to my place, and we can grill some steaks and watch the sunset?"

"That sounds nice," Sawyer mumbled drowsily. Soon she felt the even rise and fall of his chest that indicated that he had fallen asleep. Lauren tried to keep her eyes open but the combination of her lack of sleep the night before and her most recent exertions forced her to drift off.

"Mister Scott? Are you still in there?"

Lauren was startled awake when she heard the rattling of the doorknob followed by a tentative knock on his office door.

Lauren shook Sawyer and mimed for him to stay quiet and listen. In a few minutes, Elouise knocked again. "Mister Scott? Are you there?"

Sawyer, having shown himself to be adept on the fly on a previous occasion, extemporized. "Oh, I'm sorry, Miss Elouise. I had my earbuds in. I didn't hear you. Can I help you?"

"I just wanted to let you know I'm going to lunch. Can I bring you anything?"

Smirking at Lauren, he laughed and added, "No, ma'am, I have everything I need. Now, you go enjoy your lunch, Miss Elouise."

When Lauren finally emerged from Sawyer's office she looked as neatly dressed as when she'd arrived. A keen observer might have noticed, however, that there was more color in her complexion and a bit of a bounce in her step.

Jinx ambushed her the minute she returned to her classroom. "Oh my God, girl. You looked good this morning, but damn . . ."

Lauren felt her cheeks heat but didn't answer, and Jinx continued. "You didn't? Oh my God, you did! You just had sex with him, didn't you? In his office?"

Lauren still didn't answer, but she didn't have to. It was written all over her face, from the slight abrasions on her cheeks from his stubble, to the self-satisfied sparkle in her eyes.

Jinx pretended to salaam before she announced, "Oh my God, you're my hero."

Lauren, embarrassed but pleased with herself, shushed her. "Stop already, someone's going to hear you."

Jinx lowered her voice but continued to tease her. "Come on, you have to buy me lunch. I covered for you all morning. Everyone thinks you were in a new teacher meeting. So, you owe me."

"Thanks. I'll absolutely buy you lunch. Anywhere you want."

"Great. I know just the place. Come on, I'll drive."

Lauren was surprised when they pulled into the long sandy drive of Jinx's house. "I thought I was going to buy you lunch?"

"Oh, you will one day. But I thought that today, you might prefer privacy to the others asking questions."

Lauren was touched by her thoughtfulness and softly said, "Thanks, Jinx."

As they worked their way through peanut butter and jelly sandwiches and chips, Jinx asked, "Honey, I know this isn't any of my business but are you being careful?"

Lauren looked up, mouthful of peanut butter, and nodded. "*Yes, Mom*, we're being careful."

"That's not the kind of careful I mean. I mean are you being careful with your heart? You need to think about what you want from him. Is a romp in the hay every once in a while going to be enough for you, or do you want a real relationship? What does he want?"

Lauren's smile slipped a little. "We haven't really talked much," she admitted.

Peering at Lauren seriously, Jinx added, "It sounds like you're having fun, but just be careful, okay? I don't want to see you get hurt."

Lauren felt a little annoyed at Jinx for letting some of the air out of her balloon. She knew Jinx was right, though. She needed to be careful. She and Sawyer couldn't have a real relationship. It would always be one of secrets and sneaking around. *Now* that was enough for her, but would it always be? Lauren didn't want to think right now. She wanted to treasure her little bit of happiness. Changing the subject, Lauren asked, "Tell me about your fiancé."

"His name was Jack Gilbert. We met in elementary school. We were in Miss Gibbs first-grade class together."

Lauren interrupted, "Wait, isn't *Gilbert* Elouise's last name?"

"Yes, Jack was Elouise's only child."

Lauren nodded, feeling the pieces fall into place.

"Anyway, Jack was just an annoying boy I knew through elementary and middle school. Then one day in eighth grade, I looked up and he was watching me. My stomach felt all jittery and there was buzzing in my ears and that was it. I was in love."

Jinx interrupted her story to walk to the refrigerator and offer Lauren more sweet tea.

"So, what happened?"

"We dated through high school. When he got accepted at Georgia Tech and I got into Savannah College of Art and Design, we promised that we would make it work. He would drive down to SCAD or I would drive up to Atlanta. But you know what they say about long-distance relationships. It got harder and harder to find time to see each other. We still loved each other, but it was just too hard. The last time he came to Savannah to see me, I told him that we needed to break up and that the long-distance thing just wasn't working. So, we broke up."

"How sad," Lauren murmured. "That must have been terrible for you both."

"Oh, but wait, the story gets worse. Jack knew I was right. We would have eventually broken up, but he was devastated. He rushed out of my dorm and jumped in his car to drive back to Atlanta. Three hours later, Eloise called me to tell me that he had flipped his car on the interstate and been killed on impact."

"Oh, Jinx. How awful."

"I think Elouise blames me. She loves me, I know. She had assumed I would be her daughter-in-law someday. But I think that deep down some part of her blames me for his death."

"It wasn't your fault. You can't blame yourself for that," Lauren exclaimed.

"I know that. Elouise knows that. But Jack's gone, and she needs someone to blame."

Lauren and Jinx finished their sandwiches in a somber silence. Jinx dropped both plates into the dishwasher and said with a forced gaiety, "Well, time to go back to the salt mines. If you can keep it in your pants long enough, we have grade level meetings this afternoon."

"You're just jealous," Lauren said with a smirk.

"Hell yes, I'm jealous. I'll just have to live vicariously

through you," Jinx added with a grin.

"Glad I can help a sister out," Lauren teased.

Lauren spent Saturday morning shopping for her date with Sawyer—new sheets, new lingerie, new everything. She scrubbed the house from top to bottom. She bought flowers and candles. She bought and, with a little help from Jinx, assembled a new grill. She bought new chairs for the fire pit. The steaks were marinating in the refrigerator and a bottle of red wine sat ready on the countertop.

She tried to settle into some schoolwork to occupy her mind, but she couldn't focus. Eventually she gave up and headed to the beach for a long walk. She was surprised to hear the answering machine beeping when she returned two hours later hot and sweaty. Lauren felt her heart sink when she heard Sawyer's deep voice.

"Lauren, I'm so sorry. I'm going to have to cancel our date. Paula called and her car broke down. She and Molly are stranded, and I need to go get them. I was really looking forward to tonight. I'll make it up to you, I promise."

Well, what did I expect? Paula and Molly will always come first. She couldn't deny the jealousy that stung her though.

Deciding that she couldn't sit around and feel sorry for herself, Lauren called Jinx. "Hey, remember that lunch I owe you? Well I've got some expensive steaks that are going to go to waste tonight. Why don't you come over?"

"Oh, sweetie. I'm sorry things didn't work out. Should I bring some wine?"

"I've got wine, but if you have anything stronger, I think I could use it."

Lauren didn't hear from Sawyer again over the weekend. By Monday morning, she had concluded that he had changed his mind. *Maybe he's decided that he can't cheat on his wife?*

Maybe he got what he wanted from me and isn't interested anymore? Shame washed over her as she remembered her brazen seduction scene in his office. Lauren was filled with embarrassment and self-doubt as she snuck into school at the last moment on Monday morning.

Her shame was magnified when Molly rushed in bubbling with excitement. "Miss Mills, our car blew up this weekend. Steam started coming out of the engine and it made all these noises and then it just stopped right in the middle of the road!"

"Wow, Molly. That sounds like quite an adventure."

Paula, who had trailed behind Molly explained, "We blew the radiator. It could probably be fixed but Sawyer says I'd be better off just replacing the car, so he's at the dealership now."

Molly, appearing annoyed at having her story stolen, pulled on Paula's pants leg. "Are you going to ask her?"

"Ask me what, sweetheart?" *What in the world could Paula need to ask me?* Lauren felt her pulse racing. It was ridiculous, of course. Molly wouldn't be involved if Paula had found out. Paula and Molly were both smiling. *It can't be anything bad. Relax. Breathe.*

"Well, we're celebrating Sawyer's birthday tonight and Molly really wants you to come to dinner. We both really want you to come. Molly adores you, and Sawyer and I are both so grateful for how you have helped Molly."

Lauren was dumbstruck. Her mind raced. What could she possibly say? "I wouldn't want to intrude on a family event."

"Please, Miss Mills. Please, say you will come." Lauren looked from Molly's hopeful face to Paula's smiling one. She was stuck.

"Sure. I would love to come to your daddy's birthday party." Lauren's hand barely shook as she wrote down the address and offered to bring a bottle of wine. She would have to talk to Sawyer as soon as possible and get out of this somehow.

Lauren heart sank completely when Paula turned on her way out the door and added, "Oh and I almost forgot, it's a surprise, so don't say anything to Sawyer about it. Okay?"

On the inside Lauren was screaming in panic, but on the outside, she pasted on a smile and promised, "Sure, mum's the word."

As usual, her teaching occupied her complete attention for most of the day. It was only when she slowed down for snack time or outside play that Lauren had time to worry. When Jinx lined her students up for art class, Lauren was relieved to find that she was attending the party as well. *At least Jinx will be nearby to bail me out if things get awkward.*

That evening, Lauren stared into her closet in frustration. She felt like Scarlett O'Hara when Rhett Butler made her wear a red dress to Melanie's funeral. She was a hypocrite — dressing to please a man in front of his wife. Everything she chose was wrong. Eventually she compromised on a pair of flared white cotton pants and a gauzy gray tunic that flowed loosely around her. The outfit was casual but elegant, and the fabric allowed the silhouette of her figure to show. The shirt was too transparent to go without a bra, but she chose a lacy bralette that left little to the imagination. A lacy thong tugged in all the right places when she moved. She left her hair loose, falling in a silver blonde waterfall over one shoulder. Lip gloss and mascara completed her look.

Jinx let out a low whistle when Lauren arrived at the party. Under her breathe she whispered, "Sweetie, you look amazing. That poor man doesn't stand a chance."

"It's not too much, is it?" Lauren asked in a panicked voice.

"Relax. I was only teasing you. You look great."

"Miss Mills! Yay! Daddy, look Miss Mills is here." Lauren turned to see Molly hurtling across the room toward her. As she stepped forward to hug Molly, Lauren caught sight of Sawyer making his way across the room to greet her. He looked sexy as hell in a black short-sleeve polo and gray chinos. His gray eyes seemed to bore into her as he moved across the room. Lauren looked around nervously to make sure no one had noticed.

Next to her Jinx whispered, "Relax."

"Lauren, you look—" Sawyer began.

"Daddy, can I show Miss Mills my room?"

Without waiting for an answer, Molly grabbed Lauren's hand and tugged her toward the hallway. "Come on, I want to show you my dollhouse. Daddy made it for me." Lauren let the little girl lead her, acutely aware that Sawyer's gaze followed her across the room. Molly had worked her way through the names of a couple dozen stuffed animals by the time Sawyer showed up to rescue her.

"Okay, Molly, I think Miss Mills has had enough. Why don't you go see if Paula needs help with the cake?"

Placing her hands on her hips and with an indignant look on her face, Molly announced, "Daddy! You are not supposed to know about the cake."

"Sorry, sweet pea, I peeked. Don't tell on me, okay? I don't want to ruin everyone's fun."

Molly looked doubtful, but when Sawyer added the puppy dog eyes, she relented. "Okay, Daddy, I won't tell."

"Now, scoot. I need to talk to Miss Mills for a minute."

They watched together as Molly skipped back up the hall. "She'll rat me out in a heartbeat," Sawyer said as she disappeared around the corner. Turning to Lauren, he added, "I'm really sorry about the other night."

Lauren interrupted awkwardly, "It's okay. I get it. You have obligations."

"I wanted to be with you. I still do." He moved to pull her into his arms, but she slipped away from him.

"Sawyer. Not here. What if someone sees us?"

"They'll see that I'm the luckiest guy alive."

She couldn't help herself. "What about Paula?"

"Paula would be totally —" Sawyer began.

He was interrupted when Paula stuck her head in the door and announced, "Sawyer? Your presence is required in the living room."

Sawyer led the way out of the little bedroom. Lauren wasn't sure if she was imagining the odd glance from Paula as he left.

As the trio entered the living room, the crowd burst into song.

Happy birthday to you,
Happy birthday to you,
Happy birthday dear Sawyer,
Happy birthday to you.

Molly stood at a table with a huge white birthday cake in front of her. The lights had been dimmed and dozens of glowing candles flickered on top of the cake.

"Blow out the candles, Daddy. And make a wish."

Sawyer walked to the table and lifted his daughter into his arms. "Will you help me blow out the candles? Ready? One, two, three."

"Did you make a wish, Daddy?"

Sawyer pinned Lauren with his gaze as he promised his daughter, "Yes, baby girl, I made a wish."

Sawyer whispered something in his daughter's ear that sent her scampering into the kitchen with a big grin.

"I'd like to thank you all for coming tonight. We haven't been in town very long, but you have made us feel welcome. We look forward to a long and happy life here." With that, he lifted his glass in toast. Everyone else lifted the glasses of champagne that had been surreptitiously passed around.

"Now, one thing you may not realize," Sawyer continued, "is that if it's my birthday, it's also my twin sister's birthday.

Happy birthday, Paula." With that, he handed her a bouquet of pink roses that Molly had retrieved from the kitchen.

Lauren felt her glass slip through her fingers and crash on the hardwood floor. The crowd fell silent, and Lauren was sure that everybody was staring at her as she stared at the broken glass in embarrassment. "I'm so sorry." Unable to bear the attention, she abruptly muttered, "Excuse me." And she fled the room.

Sawyer found her, tears streaming down her face, in Molly's room. "What's wrong?"

Lauren turned away from Sawyer, wiping at her tears. Sawyer gripped her shoulders and turned her to face him. "Talk to me," he commanded gruffly. Then more gently he added, "Please?"

Lauren tried to keep her voice calm but as soon as she began to speak, the tears began to flow, and her questions came out in gulping sobs. "Paula's . . . your sister? You're . . . not . . . married?"

"You thought Paula and I were—that I was—" Lauren looked up abruptly as Sawyer began to laugh.

Lauren felt her heart ease and she managed a watery smile. "No, my sweet girl, I'm not married. I was. Molly's mother died when she was born. You're the first woman I have even noticed since and the only woman I plan to notice ever again. Lauren, I'm crazy about you. I have been since the moment I saw you in the bar."

When the last the party guest said goodnight, Sawyer carried a sleepy Molly to her bed. After kissing her goodnight and tucking her in, he turned to see Paula watching him.

"Why are you still here?"

"What do you mean?"

"I mean get your ass over to Miss Mill's house before she

changes her mind and I am stuck with you forever!"

"How did you—"

Paula gave him an incredulous grin. "Just go!"

Sawyer grinned and saluted. "Yes, ma'am!"

He had been certain on his drive to her house. He felt sure of himself as he walked up her shell and limestone sidewalk. But when he rang Lauren's doorbell and no one answered, he had a moment of terror. *Had he somehow misunderstood?*

Relief flooded him when he saw her round the corner of the house and smile.

"Sorry, I was on the back porch. I almost didn't hear the bell."

Anything else she intended to say was swallowed by his kiss. Without another word, she led him into the house and to her bedroom. As she reached for the light switch to turn off the lights, he stopped her. "Leave them on. I want to see you. I don't want there to be anymore misunderstandings between us." He pulled her to him and kissed her gently. His kiss deepened as she relaxed in his arms. Slowly, he began to slide his hands down her back until they rested on her firm ass. Lifting her, he pulled her against his body. She could feel every hard plane and angle of his body. She could feel his desire hard against her. She felt her body longing for his already.

"Oh, Sawyer," she moaned against his mouth.

Breaking off the kiss he led her to her bed. "Did you think of me in this bed?"

"Yes."

"Did you touch yourself and think of me?"

Shyly, she nodded.

"Will you touch yourself for me now, Lauren?"

Lauren faltered for a moment, but looking into Sawyer's

eyes, she nodded. Without another word, she stepped toward the bed and lay down. Keeping her gaze locked on his, she began to stroke her breasts. Slow circles spiraling in toward her nipples. She let out a soft moan and closed her eyes as she felt her nipples harden. She slipped her shirt off and pulled at her nipples through the sheer, lacy bralette. Rubbing the pads of her thumbs across the sensitive erect nubs, she felt herself arching in response Looking again at Sawyer, she slipped her pants off and opened her legs wide. She continued to pull at her sensitive nipples as she slid one hand between her legs. Sliding the G-string aside, she stroked her soft hot wetness. She plunged two fingers deep inside herself and then over and around the sensitive folds. Moving with excruciating slowness, she slid her fingers across the pleasurable nub. When she felt the tension in her body tightening like a spring that must release or break, she increased the pressure and speed. She could feel the moisture beading on her skin. She heard herself gasping and crying out, "Oh, Sawyer. I'm almost there. I—oh, Jesus." As she felt the spring inside her begin to release, she felt Sawyer's hands on her. His fingers deftly moved to replace hers. Just as she thought she would pitch over the abyss, he began to stroke her. She felt herself rising to a new unknown level of tension. It was like she was coming but at the same time he was working her to a new level of arousal. She felt her back arch and her body clinched and then she exploded into a million embers. She felt tears sliding down the sides of her face.

Sawyer was beside her, holding her as she writhed her way over the mountain top. Kissing the tears from her face, he sighed, "Lauren, baby, you're the most amazing woman I have ever met."

Noticing that Sawyer had removed his own clothing at some point, she smiled and said, "Hang on, baby, we're not even close to done yet." Rising gracefully, she moved her body over his and straddled him. Lifting her hips, and positioning him below her, she lowered herself onto him. She closed her eyes and felt every moment as he entered her. His cock filled her. She made her strokes long and languorous. He lifted his hips to keep her close, but she just grinned lasciviously and laughed. "Oh no, you don't."

Pulling her tight to him, he rolled them over so that he pinned her beneath him. Lowering his mouth to a nipple he drew his teeth across the sensitive surface. Hearing her soft groan, he repeated the process with the other breast. He felt her tightening below him. Her hips rocked against his in an increasing tempo. As his vision narrowed to a pinpoint and the blood rushed in his ears, he heard her cry out his name. Sawyer's world exploded. For a moment, he ceased to exist. All that existed was the glorious pleasure rippling through him. He held her against him as the waves of pleasure crested and gradually ebbed. When the world returned to them, they slept.

Later that evening, walking hand in hand along the beach, they talked. He told her about Anna's smile. He told her about trying to raise Molly alone. She told him about her parents' accident and how the Alonzos had taken her in. She told him about Nick. He had particularly enjoyed the part about accidentally saying his name.

When at last they grew quiet, they found a warm sand dune and sat, staring at the moon and its echo on the ocean's surface.

In the quiet, Lauren whispered, "What now?"

Sawyer didn't hesitate. Turning to face her, he kissed her gently. "Now my darling girl, we begin a new future — together."

You may also enjoy the following from eXtasy Books Inc:

Hot For Teacher
Kandeis Lynne

Excerpt

Whatever had passed between David and Leah the night of the dance had seemed to evaporate. David treated Leah like any other student in his class. He seemed to look right through her. And it was pissing her off!

She knew there was something powerful between them and she intended to make him face it. Step one was to give back as good as she was getting. She went back to calling him Mr. Leitner. She looked away whenever his glance skimmed over her. She did her best to pretend he didn't exist. She chatted with the other students in class, seemingly oblivious to his presence. She was certainly not oblivious—every nerve fiber in her body stood at attention when he was near. She could feel the electricity when he walked into the room—even with her back turned—but she wasn't giving in. She knew he wanted her and she was going to make him work for it.

"Okay, gang," David announced from the front of the studio, "be sure to sign up for a time before you leave tonight. You will need to show me your storyboards and lighting plans at your individual conferences."

Leah took her time gathering her things but since she sat in the front of the class and David's office was in the back, it was easy for her to manage to be the last to sign up. "Perfect!" she gloated as she scribbled her name on the last line of the sign-up sheet. "We will see how well he can ignore me when we are alone!"

To avoid acknowledging David, who had just racked the last folding chair and was headed toward his office door, Leah shouted to a friend making her way out of the studio, "Hey, wait up!" Purposely turning away from David, Leah hurried to her waiting classmate. She was certain that she heard David mumble under his breath, "Well played, Miss Leah, well played." She couldn't help but glance back once with a smirk. She saw only his back as he closed his office door.

Her storyboard conference was two days away. They were two of the longest days of her life. When the hour finally arrived, she felt like she might explode. She had spent every moment of the two days preparing for this meeting. She had spent hours on her storyboard and was justifiably proud of her effort. In any other situation she would have anticipated this meeting, looked forward to the approbation. She had always been strong academically and enjoyed the accolades that came with success. But of course, tonight that was not the only goal she had.

David cleared his throat and began, "So . . . let's see your storyboard." Leah noticed that David had strategically placed himself behind his desk and invited her to sit across from him. Point one—David.

She took the offered seat but pulled it closer to his desk, allowing her to rest her elbows on the desktop, giving him a nice view of her breasts as she leaned over the desk to explain the key elements of her presentation. Point two—Leah.

"I get this part, but can you explain how you plan to shoot

this section with only two floor cameras?"

Seizing the opportunity, Leah moved around to David's side of the desk. She could feel the heat radiating from his skin as she leaned over him to explain. Later she could not recall anything she said because all she could hear was the blood pounding in her ears. Even the smell of him set her teeth on edge.

David was equally distracted by her. He knew she was toying with him, but unfortunately it was working. Without looking at her, he ran his thumb across the space between her thumb and index finger. Time stopped. Neither of them spoke.

"You know we can't — I can't — " he growled in frustration " — I am old enough to be your father!" Finally turning to look at her, he asked, "What are you? Twelve?"

The tension relieved, Leah burst out laughing. "What are you? A hundred?"

"I'll have you know I am not one hundred — only ninety-eight! Really, how old are you?"

"Twenty," she replied.

"Jesus! Not even twenty-one! I think it would be a felony if I even kissed you!"

"Not if I let you," Leah offered, staring down at him.

"You are tempting, little Miss Leah! But as much as I would like to kiss you — and I would very much like to kiss you — I cannot. First, you are half my age. Second, you are my student. And third" — he blew out a breath — "shit, there must be a third . . ."

About the Author

Kandeis Lynne grew up in the Deep South as the proverbial preacher's kid. As a child, she lived up to the expectation; as an adult, she is living up to the reputation. A self-proclaimed hedonist, Kandeis uses her writing to explore ideas and feelings that her strict upbringing denied her. Kandeis is married, has a son, and teaches science in Tennessee.

www.ingramcontent.com/pod-product-compliance
Lightning Source LLC
Chambersburg PA
CBHW070510130626
46555CB00003B/1233